LAS BIUTY QUEENS

LAS
BIUTY
QUEENS

Iván
Monalisa
Ojeda

Introduction by Pedro Almodóvar

Translated from the Spanish by Hannah Kauders

ASTRA HOUSE | NEW YORK

Originally published in the Spanish language as
Las Biuty Queens © 2019 Alfaguara.

For information about permission to reproduce selections
from this book, please contact permissions@astrahouse.com.

Astra House
A Division of Astra Publishing House
astrahouse.com
Printed in the United States of America

Publisher's Cataloging-in-Publication Data
Names: Ojeda, Iván Monalisa, author. | Almodóvar, Pedro,
introduction. | Kauders, Hannah, translator.
Title: Las biuty queens : stories / Iván Monalisa Ojeda ; introduction by
Pedro Almodóvar ; translated from the Spanish by Hannah Kauders.
Description: New York, NY: Astra House, 2021.
Identifiers: ISBN: 9781662600302 (Hardcover) | 9781662600319 (ebook)
Subjects: LCSH Transgender people—Fiction. | Gender identity—
Fiction. | Sex workers—Fiction. | Friendship—Fiction. | New York
(N.Y.)—Fiction. | Hispanic Americans—Fiction. | Short stories,
American. | Short stories, Hispanic American (Spanish)—Translations
into English. | BISAC FICTION / Short Stories (single author) |
FICTION / Hispanic & Latino | FICTION / LGBTQ+ / Transgender
Classification: LCC PS3615.J43 B58 2021 | DDC 813.6—dc23

First edition
10 9 8 7 6 5 4 3 2 1

Design by Richard Oriolo
The text is set in Century Schoolbook.
The titles are set in Avenir LT Std 85 Heavy.

Contents

Introduction by Pedro Almodóvar | 1

Overdose | 5

In the *Bote* | 11

Ortiz Funeral Home | 41

Jennifer's Carnations | 51

Adriana la Chimba, or
The Gorgeous Adriana de Pereira | 59

Emergency Room | 69

Biuty Queen | 93

Little Miss Lightning Bolt | 99

The Boricua's Blunts | 107

Lorena the Chilena | 123

A Coffee Cup Reading | 133

Mother Hen and Her Chicks | 145

Sabrina's Wedding | 153

LAS BIUTY QUEENS

Introduction

⁓⧓⁓

THE STORY COLLECTION in your hands may sound like a book about transvestites and queer people, and that's what it is, but it's more than just that. Monalisa is Chilean, and in these stories he/she narrates the day-to-day, or rather, the night-to-night, of a group of Latinx transgender people and transvestites who work the streets, prostituting themselves in bars and in not-to-be-recommended back alleys in New York City. The American dream—seen from the height of a good pair of heels—turns into a nightmare, an everyday nightmare. For these *biuty queens*, violent death comes with the territory. The stories could be very sordid, but Iván Monalisa has the talent to endow his/her characters with vitality and grace: he/she tells you about their misery as something inevitable, but with humor and without turning them into victims. These are stories of survival in the face of Trump's immigration policies, with characters who skirt urban dangers with humor and solidarity. They share drugs, pimps, beauty contest awards, illness, and delirium, but they are a very close-knit community.

They remind me of my mother's neighbors, when she went to live back in her hometown during her final years. Her neighbors took care of her much better than we would have. The solidarity and care among the widows who lived on my mother's street is one of the most beautiful things I remember of my hometown. It is not strange that Julieta Serrano told her son that she didn't want him to include her neighbors in his films. Neighbors are sacred, in the full meaning of that word.

They're not entirely similar, but *Las Biuty Queens* reminds me of my book of stories about Patty Diphusa—they show very different human landscapes and social surroundings. Mine is all hedonist fiction, while the stories in *Las Biuty Queens* radiate realism in every sentence.

—*Pedro Almodóvar*

Overdose

NIGHT FALLS. I haven't slept in three days. My pupils are dilated and my eyes are red. Sprawled out on the bed, almost motionless, I'm convinced my body smells of ether.

When I turn out the lights in my room, everything falls into shadows. Little by little, piles of clothing start to take human shape. Immobile forms everywhere I turn. As night draws on, they look more and more like the silhouettes of people. It must be the effect of not having closed my eyes in days.

It's the middle of summer, and the room I'm renting is on the third floor of a house in the Bronx. A house made of wood that holds in all the heat. I don't have air-conditioning and the fan does nothing to regulate the rising temperature of my body. I sweat something that smells like chemicals and artificial sweetener.

I have a big bottle of water next to my bed, but I can't bring myself to move, not even to reach for a drink. It doesn't matter that I haven't had a drop of water in over ten hours.

My intestines feel all crunchy because my stomach is empty, but I'm not hungry. I have enough money to order delivery, but something keeps me from picking up the phone. I can't let anyone hear my voice. The last time I made a call on my cell, my friend asked what was going on, why my voice sounded all metallic, like I was calling from beyond the grave.

Calling 9-1-1 isn't an option. I know from experience that nothing good can come of it. First they'll cart me off to the emergency room, and then straight to the psych ward at Bellevue.

I pick up the rosary just as I always have since the age of ten whenever I feel rage or fear coming on. I try to pray, but I don't have the patience. I barely make it through seven Ave Marias.

I get used to the dark. I can distinguish between objects, but I can't let my eyes focus on anything in particular. I know that, if I do, I'll see someone.

Without wanting to, I look toward the closet. The door's cracked open. I make out a pair of shoes, and then, all of a sudden, the shoes are attached to a pair of legs. There's someone inside my closet. I can see him clearly. He has long legs. I sit up in bed and whisper to him to leave me alone.

Then I see my silk kimono shining in the semidarkness. It's draped over a suitcase. In a second, it transforms before my eyes into the silhouette of a woman who is facedown, kneeling. I can't bear to look at her face. I squeeze my eyes shut.

I lie back down on the bed, which is damp and has a sweet smell. I take a deep breath and decide to start opening my eyes very, very slowly. On the opposite end of the bed, just beyond my feet, the only window in the room opens onto a giant tree that must be over a century old. A faint wind rustles its branches. Little by little, the swaying starts to accelerate and I hear what sounds like voices repeating an unintelligible mantra.

I close my eyes again and try to breathe deeply. Something tells me it's all in my head, or it must be the effect of so many sleepless nights.

I try to snap out of it. I look for the bottle of water at the foot of the bed. I'm not thirsty, but I know I should drink something. I feel better. Better than I've felt in many hours.

I promise myself this really will be the last time. I pull the glass pipe out from under my pillow and open the little plastic bag of crystal meth. I empty some of it into the pipe. I take the lighter and begin heating up the glass bulb. When I see the white smoke building up in the center of the bulb, I take a long hit. I repeat this four times. I wait for the pipe to cool down and put it back under the pillow.

I lie faceup on the bed. I think of the time I told a friend that whenever I'm high on crystal meth and haven't slept for a few days, I start seeing human forms. This isn't the first time. My friend said they must be the ghosts of people who overdosed. Looking me straight in the eye, she warned me never to talk to the shadows, never to make any kind of contact with them. I should ignore them. It was for my own good, she said. I close my eyes and try to get them out of my head. But suddenly, everything starts spinning very slowly, in a way that feels almost pleasant, until just as suddenly, everything falls still.

I muster the courage to sit down on the edge of the bed. I open my eyes and look toward the closet with the open doors. There are the shoes, which now connect to a pair of legs and the shadow of a man. I whisper to him without fear. I tell him this can't be real, that what I'm seeing is no ghost. I ask if he's really there, but the shadow doesn't reply. I say it over and over again until I hear a voice saying no, none of us are dead. We are only shadows. I turn my head to see who's speaking. My kimono is still being worn by the woman who, just a moment ago, was kneeling, facedown. Now she's raised her head. I can't help but stare. She tells me not to worry. Not to be afraid. She tells me to lie down and try to close my eyes. It's time to rest. They'll watch over me as I dream. And then the voices disappear and with them go all the colors.

In the *Bote*

❧

THE POLICE HAD STOPPED ME on multiple occasions.
The last time was around two months before what
I'm about to tell you.

After leaving the bar, if I hadn't made enough money,
I'd go walking along 14th Street toward 9th Avenue. My
friend La Maru lived close by in the Chelsea projects.
That's where I'd change from him into her or from her into
him. So *taco, taquito, tacón, Iris Chacón*. I'd wait to see if

anything happened, if any cars showed up. Can you give me a ride? If they said yes, I'd get in. And even if I couldn't get any money out of them, they'd at least give me a ride. The most they'd do was try to touch my legs on the way. I'd ask them if they wanted anything more. If they wanted to play, they should at least give me a tip. If they said no, *pues okay, babe, thanks for the ride.* Leave me here.

One of those nights, almost at the end of the fall, I was doing shows at a bar downtown, one of the many run by the legendary Sandy Michelle. I had to play Bette Midler. So songs like "I'm Beautiful" or "One Monkey Don't Stop No Show" were part of my repertoire. They paid me fifty bucks and gave me open bar. Of course, I always ended up drunk.

As on so many other nights, I walked along 14th Street to 9th Avenue. As I started to cross 8th Avenue, a car pulled up next to me. The window on the driver's side rolled down and a sixty-something man appeared. He had pink cheeks and a full white beard.

"Hi, babe. What's up? Want to get in?"

I stood there looking at him. Despite his appearance, and even though Christmas was fast approaching, he obviously wasn't Santa Claus. I thought in silence about his red snapper face on the streets of New York.

"Can you give me a ride?"

"Sure, babe. Hop in."

There's money here, I thought as I climbed in. We hadn't even made it half a block when a patrol car stopped us. Two officers told me to get out and handcuffed me without another word. I tried to justify myself, saying I'd just asked him for a ride, but I was already prepared to get into the police car.

The officers went over to talk to my alleged driver. Turns out Santa Claus was undercover. A plainclothes cop.

It went the same as always, the same as so many times before. They took me to the police station on 14th Street, in New York's sixth precinct. When they loaded me into the van, it was almost full already. Nothing out of the ordinary, since it was almost five in the morning. The last time an undercover cop caught me, I was the first one in the van. It wasn't even ten at night, so I had to wait more than four hours for the van to fill up. One by one, they picked up my colleagues, girls they arrested at the exits of strip clubs or who worked in bars. Lots of them had gone over to the undercover cops giving them the whole sexy fool act. *Babe, do you want a lap dance?* They'd leave with what they thought was a john, and right there in the middle of the street, the police would be waiting. They'd put her in handcuffs and load her straight up into the van.

But this time, I was the last person aboard the ship. No waiting, straight to the precinct. Nothing left to do but kill time until they took you to be sentenced.

The first time they arrest you for prostitution, the sentence is to attend a class on safe sex, followed by another on the use of narcotics. When they catch you a second time, they start giving you days of community service: two days cleaning a park or putting stamps on mail at the NYPD offices. The more times they catch you, the more days of community service you get. Once, my friend La Myriam Hernández from El Salvador had to do a whole month of community service.

I saw all this coming, but there was still something about it that surprised me. A few years before that night, in 2000 to be exact, I'd decided to walk the streets more. Years of hard-core hustling. I always made money or at least got a ride up to Washington Heights, where I lived at the time. From the center of the action down on 14th Street all the way uptown was a long way, but the cars would hop on the West Side Highway and get there in a flash. I walked the streets at least three days a week. Or, I should say, three nights.

Hustling on 14th Street in those years was like being right in the lion's den. Or, rather, in the police's den, because they're one and the same. They were always out patrolling. They knew everything that went on and would arrest you if they felt like it. They were always there, always on the prowl.

After the first month, when those bohemian cobblestone streets finally felt familiar under my heels, just when I'd learned to walk on them almost effortlessly, I started getting caught. They arrested me five times in three months.

Sometimes they'd catch me when I was inside the car, just as the john on call was handing me the cash. Other times, they'd arrest me just for being in the area. *You should thank us, we were waiting for you to make your money*, that hypocrite of a lieutenant Torres said to me once. He was in charge of arresting all the sex workers he found walking around his territory. Once he arrested me just for talking to a man I asked for the time. Three patrol cars pulled up in front of me. With all the paraphernalia and the commotion, I thought they must have confused me with some high-risk criminal. Six police officers must have gotten out. I was cornered like a stray cat, blinded by the lights and somewhat stunned by the sound of the sirens. I'd never felt so important.

It happened so many times and I got so many sentences of community service that, after a while, I started forgetting about the days when I was supposed to be cleaning parks or sweeping streets, and even the days when I had hearings with the judge.

To get myself out of all this, I decided not to go back to hooking on the streets. From then on, I'd only work in bars. Case closed, I thought. I didn't know back then and wouldn't know until this arrest that your absences from community service or hearings turn into guarantees. This means if the police arrest you again, you go straight to jail. To Rikers Island, I mean. Or *Las Rocas*, "the rocks," as Latinos call it.

Normally I'd wait anxiously for the moment when I'd go to court to see the judge, but this time, I wanted the time to pass slowly. I just had this feeling. Maybe that's why I came up with the brilliant idea of giving them a different name from the one I'd used before. The first time they arrested me, a *loca* in the van gave me some advice. I should never use my real name. The best thing was to say you were Puerto Rican. That way no one would bother to check if you were legal or illegal. Boricuas are citizens. And when it came to my Social Security number, I should say I'd forgotten it, obviously. The police think we're all on drugs and have no idea what's going on around us. That's why, since my first arrest, I'd been calling myself Juan Cruz. Why Juan? Why Cruz? Beats me. This time, on my way to the courthouse in Midtown, handcuffed in the back of the van, I decided to call myself Luis Rivera. What could be more Puerto Rican than Luis? What was more Boricua than Rivera?

But as soon as I got to the courthouse, everything turned against me from the moment they took my fingerprints. They didn't use ink anymore. That horrible stain that stayed on your fingers for days as a reminder: *te arrestaron por puta*. They arrested you for being a whore. Well, not anymore. Gone were the days of ink pads. We were in a new millennium. Now you had to press the tips of your fingers to a screen that recorded your prints digitally.

"Name?" the officer asked me.

"Luis Rivera," I answered confidently.

I waited to see some kind of reaction on his face as he entered my name. For him to realize that the names didn't match up. I thought he must be used to lying delinquents, because that reaction never came.

Once all the paperwork was done, they returned me

to a cell in the courthouse and I waited to be seen by a judge. After a few minutes, the attorney who was going to represent me arrived, a fifty-something white man. He sat down across from me and started to read my record.

"Hmm," he murmured as he read my criminal history. "Are you Mr. Cruz or Mr. Rivera?"

Back then, people didn't have the delicacy to ask you for your preferred pronouns. So his *mister* sounded dry and direct.

"Call me whatever you like, I'm both," I answered with a smirk.

He gave me a look that wasn't quite a smile. He needed to maintain his composure.

"I see that your only arrests have been for prostitution. Let's hope the judge will be benevolent with his sentence."

As soon as he said this, he looked back over my record and let out an exclamation.

"Yes?" I said, nervous.

"It says here you didn't show up for your community service twice. And on another occasion, you missed your hearing with the judge. A hearing you requested yourself, as you were pleading not guilty. The judge threw you a bone by giving you another court date to prove you were innocent. And you didn't show up?"

"I know," I replied.

"This means you now have three guarantees. A guarantee signifies lack of respect for the law. But like I was saying, you've only been arrested for prostitution. No violent crime or anything like that. I'll see you in just a moment."

He stood up, gave me a serious look, and left.

I waited for my turn to go in for my hearing, praying I'd have good luck with the judge.

Then a police officer appeared and escorted me to the courtroom. The moment they opened the door, I heard a voice say:

"Juan Cruz also known as Luis Rivera."

That was me. Juan Cruz also known as Luis Rivera. What a criminal you are, *loca*, I thought to myself. You even have an alias. They took off my handcuffs and sat me down next to the attorney. I felt him looking at me with a restrained smile. It wasn't enough to promise the judge I'd do all the community service he wanted. The judge, who had a face like a friendless dog, wouldn't let his arm be twisted: he gave me three months in *Las Rocas* and, at the end of February, another hearing. Or five thousand for bail. That was the irrevocable sentence.

From the courthouse, they took me to Central Booking,

also known as the Tombs, because it was located in a sort of basement under another, bigger courthouse in Chinatown. Calling it a tomb seemed accurate—it never saw the light of day. I was in a cell there for hours. Until I heard the call that I would hear repeated so many times: Juan Cruz also known as Luis Rivera.

I stood up. An officer took me down a long hall that led outside, where a bus with bars at the windows was waiting for me. I climbed into that jail cell on wheels, which was full in less than fifteen minutes. I looked around at my travel companions. I saw frustrated expressions all over the place, but I also saw so many faces of guys who were used to all this.

An armored door separated us from the driver. We were all handcuffed. I felt the buzz of motors and far-off voices. Through the window, I could see several identical buses approaching ours. Armored buses that transported the crème de la crème from every county in New York City: Staten Island, Queens, the Bronx, Brooklyn, and, of course, Manhattan, were represented among those who washed up. They made us climb out and go into one of the two stations in front of us. They were made of cement-colored bricks. Men came and went, all in gray or orange jumpsuits. Of the people who passed me, 80 percent were prisoners. The rest, guards and police officers. I don't know how so few people can control so many.

They put me in a line. Almost three days had passed since I got arrested because of that fucking Santa Claus. My makeup had worn off, with the exception of my waterproof mascara. I hadn't spent those ten dollars in vain. The rest of the makeup I'd stolen, of course. Three days without showering, three days without shaving. In sum, I was a bewigged queen who looked like Freddy Krueger. I waited my turn. An inmate crossed in front of me. I was shocked by the color of his skin, a complexion so white it must not have seen the sun in years. Skin that became almost transparent under the lights of the shed. Then it was my turn. They made me go into a big room that looked like the bathroom of a dilapidated athletic center.

They told me to take off my clothes. The wig was the first thing I took off. Next came my shoes and everything else. I couldn't believe I'd been wearing heels the whole time. Until that moment, I hadn't even noticed.

They put all my things into a big paper bag. When I was ready to get in the shower, the inmates who had been there for a long time and were in charge of these procedures started to play with my nipples, which were hard because of my sporadic experiences with female hormones and how cold it was in that place. To one of them—who was pretty handsome, I might add—I gave a look like *touch whatever you want, babe.* We smiled at each other. And before I could start to dream that he was my husband in there, the time came for me to get in the shower.

I had just three minutes. Those had to be the three most enjoyable minutes of the last few days. I had to put on the orange uniform and matching slip-ons. All of us were silent. Tired. A long vacation at Rikers Island Resort awaited us.

After the shower, they drove us over to another building. The one that housed the dormitories. It was a spacious place, with around fifty or sixty beds. There was a guard in a barred cubicle with a window looking onto the dormitory. He communicated with inmates through the window.

I'd just entered when someone came up to me. He was a white man with a brown beard, around my height. He said hello and welcomed me. Surprised, I said hi back. I sensed a Latino accent, so I asked where he was from. And because I'd had enough of lying about my origins, I answered him:

"I'm from Chile. From the South of South America."

"Oh, a Chilean one!" he exclaimed. "There's another guy from Chile here. Do you want me to introduce you?"

"No, please. I don't want to meet any Chilean guys. I came here from my country a long time ago. And honestly, I'm not in the mood for Chileans. Now less than ever."

I'd just finished my sentence when they announced lights-out. Time for bed.

I hadn't had any time to get settled, so I lay down in the first empty bed I could find. I threw myself down and, with no blanket to warm me, started to shiver from the cold. In complete darkness, I asked my neighbors in the next beds over for something to keep me warm. Someone told me to ask the guard in the cubicle. So I, rather sure of myself, called out into the darkness:

"Guard. Please, I need a blanket."

"Who's talking?"

"Juan Cruz also known as Luis Rivera. I need something to keep warm."

"It's the end of my shift. I'll let the next guard know."

"Thank you, sir," I replied, getting used to my surroundings.

I lay shivering from the cold. Suddenly, I heard a voice.

"Hey, did you just get here?"

"Yes, it's my first time."

"Here, take this."

He tossed over something heavy and furry that fell on top of me. I could barely see my neighbor in the darkness of the dorm. I wrapped myself up in the blanket.

As I was beginning to fall asleep, I heard, "Where's Juan Cruz?"

"Right here."

"Do you need a blanket?"

"No, thanks. Somebody gave me one."

He'd probably seen on my record that I was a lady of the night, along with the photo in my file and the reason for my arrest.

Loudly, he said, "Ah, I see how it is. Traded it for a blow job, right?"

The silence suddenly erupted into shouts of mockery, contempt, and shock. I didn't have the energy to think or react. I fell asleep.

All of a sudden, I sensed voices and movement. Light invaded the space. I was so tired that everyone, or almost everyone, had gotten up before me. I sat up in bed and tried to find the face of the person who'd welcomed me.

My bed was in the middle of so many beds. I was in the

middle of so many people. Lots of them were walking in the same direction, toward the bathroom, I assumed.

I spotted my neighbor. He was walking in my direction. I greeted him enthusiastically as he walked by. He looked over and immediately looked away. He walked right by me. Before I let myself feel too surprised by his reaction, I remembered what had happened the night before. Everyone knew that a *loca* had arrived. I went over to the guard's station, which now had a woman in it. I asked her for a towel. Without looking at me, she handed me one, along with a small bar of soap. An African American man gave me a shove with his shoulder, all tough-guy, *get out of my way*. I looked all around me. The showers were empty. I was on high alert. I showered quickly. I didn't even use soap. I returned to my bed. I threw myself onto it. It was my territory, the only place where I could feel safe and, dare I say it, protected.

In the adjoining room, they switched on a huge TV mounted on the ceiling. A group of Chinese men were playing chess. I sat up and walked over to them, miming *hey, let's play*. But they, too, ignored me.

Then an announcement came over the loudspeaker that it was time to go out to the yard. I wanted to stay in the dormitory.

The prisoners returned from their jaunt. Nobody looked at me. Nobody said hello. Everyone split into groups. White people with other white people, Boricuas with other *morenos*. The Chinese guys ignored one another. The Mexicans had their own group off to the side.

I realized there was an empty bed right across from the guard's station. An instinct, maybe one of survival, sent me running over to it like a shot. I asked the guard if the bed belonged to anyone. *Empty and available*, she replied indifferently.

I took my blanket over and settled in. From then on, that spot was my refuge. It would be harder for anyone to do something to me if the guards were watching. Once again, everyone got up from their beds. From their little homes. I assumed it was lunchtime. I was so hungry I could have eaten a whole cow.

I stood at the back of the line. As we moved through the halls, other lines of prisoners joined ours. We had to walk between the wall and a white line on the floor. To step over the line was enough to make the guards bark at you like furious dogs.

I heard one inmate say it was his first time in jail and he didn't know he was supposed to walk inside the line. He didn't get to finish his sentence. Two police officers threw themselves on top of him. Once they had him on the floor, they handcuffed him and dragged him back to the dorms.

"An extra lunch!" yelled someone in line.

We all started laughing.

In the cafeteria, I took a plastic tray. Other prisoners who had to work in the kitchen that day were in charge of serving the food. Pasta, juice, bread, and an orange. I sat down at a random table. The pasta, which had no tomato sauce on it, got clogged in the middle of my throat. It was viscous, unswallowable. The guy sitting next to me asked me if I was going to eat it. I said no. He grabbed my plate and devoured the pasta.

I saved the orange for myself. I ate it slowly, trying to imagine it was a hamburger or something like that. I ended up drinking the juice. I can't remember what kind it was, but I liked it; it was sweet and refreshing.

When I finished eating, a white man in his early thirties sat down across from me. He was so attractive that I can still see him perfectly. He looked around as he ate, like someone was after him. He had a teardrop tattoo under his left eye. Later on, I learned this means you've killed someone. Every tear is a kill on your record.

His presence terrified and fascinated me. He left as soon as he finished eating. Maybe he was being chased by the spirit of the dead he carried with him in the form of that teardrop. As my misfortune or luck would have it, I never saw him again.

A guard announced that lunch was over.

Back to the line, again. Back to marching between the white line and the wall. Once I was back in the dormitory, I got settled in my new place, in the bed across from the guard who looked over us. I didn't want to lie down. I stayed seated. I started to blame myself: this is what you get for being a *loca estúpida*. You knew they'd get you sooner or later. What would it have taken to just show up for your hearing and ask for forgiveness? They would've given you a month of community service and fined you less than a hundred bucks. But no. Bonehead. Look where it got you. A cage.

I was almost ready to throw myself onto the bed and surrender to depression when I heard a voice with a familiar accent.

"Hey, *vos soi chileno*?"

I lifted my head and saw a face smiling at me. A face that reminded me of some classmate from school or other.

Of some neighbor. Of some friend of a friend. It was the very same person that I, in my arrogance, had refused to meet.

"Hi. Yes. I'm Chilean," I answered with a mix of joy and gratitude.

"Can I sit down?"

"Of course."

He took a seat and continued.

"What's your name?"

Tired of false names, I told him the truth.

"Iván."

"I'm Vladimir."

He sat there looking at me, as though he was waiting for me to ask him something. When I didn't say anything, he continued:

"I know. Vladimir isn't a very common name in Chile. It's just that my dad was a communist. And he loved anything that sounded Russian. My name is Vladimir and I have two younger siblings, Igor and Tatiana." He thought for a moment and looked at me. "Wait, but you have a Russian name, too! Iván."

"Yes," I said, smiling. He seemed like a really nice guy. "But my dad isn't a communist. What are you in for?"

"My vices," he answered.

"What do you mean?"

"They caught me buying heroin. I've been here three months. At least I've been able to get clean. They give me methadone, so the cravings don't get too bad. When I got here, I didn't sleep for four days. My bones hurt so much all I could do was scream. But then, on the fifth day, they gave me methadone. And from then on, *tranqui, tranquiléin*. What about you? Why are you here?"

"I let a few guarantees add up."

"Oh!" he said, realizing I didn't want to tell him why I got arrested. He stood up. "You look a little tired. Take a nap and I'll come back in a while."

"Cool."

I stretched out in my bed. A pleasant warmth washed over my body. I took a nap. I know I slept with a smile on my face.

I don't know how much time passed. All I know is that I heard a voice waking me up.

"Psst, hey."

I opened my eyes and saw my new friend.

"Check it out. I have tea and cookies. Snack time!"

I sat up like a shot, fighting the urge to hug him. I contained myself. I felt happy.

Once again, he asked with ceremony if he could sit down. Without saying anything, I moved over to make space for him to sit.

He sat down and put the tea bag into a plastic cup full of hot water.

"This is enough for two."

"How Chilean is this?" I replied, laughing.

"These even look like Tritón cookies. Eight of them. Four for you and four for me."

The cookies were like a Coca-Cola in the middle of the desert. I devoured them.

"When do you get out?" he asked me.

"At the end of February. I could get out sooner if I paid bail."

"How much is it?"

"Five thousand dollars," I told him, blowing on the hot water in my plastic cup, which had started to turn the color of tea. "As you can probably imagine, I have no money."

"All you have to pay is five hundred."

"No, I said five thousand."

"Yeah, but you only have to pay 10 percent of the bail. If it's five thousand, you only pay five hundred."

"Really?" I asked him, shocked, scarfing down the last of the cookies meant for Vladimir.

"Totally. My bail is ten thousand. So I only have to pay a thousand. I called my ma to get her to pay it, but she said no, I'll be better off staying here until I've been clean for a few months. She said maybe it'll clear my mind and I won't do drugs again." He took a deep breath and continued. "I think she's right, *cachái*? Mothers are always right."

"How'd you call her?" I asked, incredulous and excited at the same time. "You don't have a cell phone in here, do you?"

"Man, you can tell it's your first time. See the telephone over there on the wall next to the bathroom?"

He pointed toward a phone identical to the public ones all over the streets of New York.

"All inmates have a right to two calls a day." He paused to pick up the two empty cups. "Well, I think it's almost lights-out. I'll see you tomorrow, Iván. Good night."

"Wait! Do you think I could call now?"

"Sure, but you should hurry. They're about to turn the lights off."

I got to the phone in a flash. I didn't have a cell phone back then, so I knew all my friends' numbers by heart. I called La Maru, my friend from the Chelsea projects, the last person I'd seen. It didn't even ring twice before she answered.

"Hi, Maru? It's me."

"Oh my god!" she yelled from the other side. "Where are you? What happened?"

"Just here in the *bote*, as Mexicans say."

"We were all going ballistic. La Silvia and La Manuel have been acting crazy. They won't stop calling to see if I've heard from you."

"Well tell them to get together five hundred dollars so I can get out of here. They need to go to the courthouse on Centre Street and give my name, and they'll tell them what to do. La Silvia knows all this by heart."

"Okay. I can't promise you anything, but the good thing is that you're—"

"Alive," I said before she could finish the sentence.

"La Silvia was ready to start looking for you at the morgue."

"Tell that queen I'm still kicking."

All of a sudden, I heard a whistle. The warning that the call was about to end. Quickly I told La Maru, "When they go to pay my bail, tell them to ask about Juan Cruz also known as Luis Rivera. Remember that. Juan Cruz, Luis Rivera—"

I'd just finished saying it when the call got cut off.

When I went back to my bed, the guard was giving the lights-out. Time to sleep.

"Thank you, Vladimir!" I said loudly, laid out in my bed.

"You're welcome," he replied from the darkness.

A few days passed like that. A week, maybe. Vladimir always showed up with tea and Tritón-style cookies at six in the evening. He got along so well with all the inmates that everyone started talking to me, even coming up to say hi. And I started feeling comfortable, maybe even a little *too* comfortable.

Once, when I was resting in my bed, I heard Vladimir's voice.

"Hey, Iván, come over here."

"What's up?" I replied from my bed-home.

"Just come over here and I'll tell you."

I stood up and saw that he was standing a few beds away, talking to another inmate. I walked over to them.

"This is Carlos. He's the boss in this dorm. Anything you need, any problem or whatever, always talk to him," Vladimir said, with his characteristic formality.

Carlos was a gray-haired man around fifty. He was tall and thin. I knew without being told that he was Boricua. He held out his hand and I gave him mine.

"Nice to meet you. I'm Iván."

He didn't say anything. He just reached out his hand and gave me the once-over.

I always felt so safe and comfortable in Vladimir's company that I sat right down on Carlos's bed, planning to chat him up and charm him with a little attitude.

I noticed Carlos turning all sorts of colors. The colors of rage. Without knowing what was going on, I looked at Vladimir, who'd gone white as a sheet and had his eyes wide open like plates. Silently, he grabbed my arm and pushed me toward my bed.

"Lie down and don't move. Don't say anything. Don't even breathe. Let me figure out how to fix this."

I realized it was serious and I was afraid. Carlos was yelling.

"I'm gonna teach that guy some respect. That *pato's* finished."

A cold sweat dripped down my back. I didn't understand what was happening. I heard Vladimir's voice and could tell from his tone that he was trying to calm Carlos down. Other prisoners got out of bed to see what was going on. The boss had lost his mind. Someone had pissed him off. And that someone was me. But I still didn't know what my mistake had been. I heard Carlos start to lower his voice a bit. Vladimir didn't stop talking to him. Didn't stop calming him down. I buried my head in my pillow. I could sense that Vladimir was talking to me. He sat down at my side.

"Never lie down or even sit on a bed that isn't yours. The only thing we have here is our beds. It's our only property. Not even the guards bother us when we're in bed, so don't you go trying it again. Now get up and go apologize to him."

I got up out of bed, and with the utmost seriousness, I approached the leader. He sat back and waited for me to deliver my apology.

"I am so sorry, sir. I've never been in jail before and I'm not familiar with the codes of conduct. Please accept my sincerest apologies."

When I saw he wasn't saying anything, I started to tremble.

"All right. Just don't let it happen again."

I thanked him and went back to my bed. Vladimir shot me a gesture of approval. I tried to thank him by mouthing the words. That night, I fell asleep right away. I knew he'd saved me from something dangerous.

As soon as I woke up the next day, I looked for Vladimir. I found him hunched over in his bed. I asked him what was wrong.

"Stomachache and nausea. This methadone is just as bad as heroin, if not worse. I think I'm going to the infirmary."

"Want some company?

"You're joking, right? Don't you know where you are? No one keeps anyone else company here." He took a deep breath and stood up. "I'll see you tomorrow. They'll probably keep me overnight, until it passes."

"Good luck," I said.

I lay back down in bed. I didn't go out to the yard. I preferred to wait inside until lunch. I entertained myself by staring up at the ceiling.

That's when I heard a voice say, "Juan Cruz also known as Luis Rivera."

I didn't react, so the guard repeated my name.

"That's me."

Without even looking at me, the guard continued.

"Take your things. You're leaving today. They paid your bail."

I didn't know what to do. I was frozen.

"What are you waiting for? Clock's ticking. Get your stuff or I'm leaving you here another day."

I ran to the guard's station. I didn't have anything to take with me. I asked him if we could stop by the infirmary so I could say goodbye to my friend. He looked at me disapprovingly and didn't answer.

The whole process of leaving took about as long as entering. I put on normal clothes, whatever I could find that was my size in the box they gave me. There weren't any shoes, so I left wearing the slip-ons. On the bus, they gave me a subway card. It took me a few hours to get to La Maru's house.

I slept for almost two days straight. I knew I couldn't get caught again, at least not before my hearing with the judge in February. I tried to make money miming in subway stations. I'd set up at Columbus Circle, Times Square, and sometimes Bedford Avenue. I'd stand there for hours. I never saw any person in particular. What I saw was a collective human blob. One day, I thought I recognized a figure when I heard a coin fall into my hat. I opened my eyes wide, but all I saw was a mass of people rushing by. Two boys were sitting on a bench on the platform, sharing a bag of cookies. I went back to my routine. I returned to my miming until I was sure I caught a whiff of tea. I listened to the boys laugh, far off, like an echo. I paused and once more, in silence, gave thanks for my Chilean friend Vladimir.

Ortiz Funeral Home

SLEEP TOO MUCH, FOR A CHANGE. I take the downtown A express to get to 14th Street as quickly as possible. As soon as I exit the station, I feel a hot gust of air, a drastic change from the strong air-conditioning of the subway car. It's the middle of summer and I'm walking fast. All of a sudden, I see it in front of me: Ortiz Funeral Home. I collect myself before climbing the stairs. In one gulp, I finish my bottle of water. I concentrate on acting appropriately for the occasion. And the occasion is a wake. I open the door to the funeral home and am overcome by an ice-cold gust of air and the scent of flowers. I feel grateful. On a list propped up on a lectern, I search for the name of the deceased. Finally, I see it. *José Buchillon also known as Amalia, la cubana, room four.*

When I feel ready to go in and pay my respects, I hear someone call my name.

"Monalisa!"

It's La Manuel, her face bathed in tears. I go over to embrace her.

"*Ay, bendito,* Amalia's in a better place."

"I know that," she replies. "That's not why I'm crying,"

"Then what's wrong?"

"These *locas* have the nerve to say I stole the bag of coke."

"What?"

"The bag of cocaine they put in Amalia's hands so she could take it with her to the great beyond," she says, drying her tears. "You know how fond she was of that sweet little powder. But can you believe they're saying I stole it? Ungrateful *maricas.* How many times have I bought them drugs when they were broke? I've done it for more than a few of the ones who are now pointing their fingers at me."

And she starts to cry again.

"*Ay*, *loca*, please. It's not a big deal."

As soon as I say this, La Manuel stops crying. She shoots me a look, blows her nose, and interjects, "You have to understand that losing Amalia hasn't been easy on me. Wait here, I'm going to the bathroom."

And just like that, she disappears.

While I wait, I examine a poster-size photograph on the wall next to a door. It's Amalia's portrait. Under her face is a caption that reads *R.I.P.* The image shows Amalia, her face that *mulata* shade of cinnamon, wearing long false lashes and a wedding-style hat in a hue like *café con leche*. A wide-brimmed hat. Very wide. Elegant, I think. I remember seeing her do a show at Sally's. She was singing that La Lupe song "Puro Teatro." Tall and *mulata*, my friend Amalia from Cuba always stood out. La Manuel always said she was loaded. That she wore a new outfit every night and, most importantly, new shoes. And you'd better believe it was no small feat to find a size-twelve shoe for that Caribbean foot.

La Manuel's return rouses me from those memories.

"Okay, I'm ready."

I look at her and see her eyes bulging.

"Mm-hmm!" I exclaim as she blows her nose.

"Mm-hmm, it's time. Let's go say a proper hello to Amalia," she says, with a look of suspicion that matches my own.

As La Manuel opens the door to the room where the wake is being held, I remember a phrase I heard once in a Narcotics Anonymous meeting. *We addicts are masters in fooling people.* As soon as I walk in, I see Diva de Panamá sitting beside the casket. Close friend of the deceased, she plays the role of a family member receiving condolences. I look at her with curiosity. Of course she's wearing the hat I just saw in the portrait by the entrance. La Manuel guesses what I'm thinking and whispers into my ear:

"It's not just the hat, she kept the business, too. Some people are even saying she kept the drugs," she adds before leaving me on my own.

I go up to Diva to offer my condolences.

"Monalisa, hi. Thanks for coming," she says, her voice full of sadness.

"*Ay*, of course, *niña*. She's in a better place," I say, not looking at the casket. I've never liked to look the dead in the face. I give Diva a hug.

"These *locas* have no respect for anything or anyone," she says slowly, rubbing her nose.

"Yes, I know. They took her bag of coke out of the casket."

"Oh, you already heard?"

"La Manuel told me. And she's really hurt that they've accused her of stealing it."

"No," says Diva, arranging herself in her seat. "She's only one of the suspects. No one's accused her directly."

As I walk away, I notice that her nose is running. I say hi to some people I know, which accounts for almost everyone in the room. I'm overhearing phrases like "I still can't believe it," "She's in a better place," and "Wasn't she wonderful," when the doors open and someone cries out.

"Leave me alone. Please, just leave me alone!"

It's Lorena the Chilena. Also known as Hugo Loren. We all get out of her way. She walks straight up to the casket. She stands in front of the deceased and, from the small purse hanging around her neck, removes a bag of coke. She opens it ceremoniously and does a bump.

"To you!" she says, sneezing.

She leans into the body and starts whispering into her ear. I hear someone ask if it's the same bag that went missing.

"Was it La Lorena who took it?"

"No, no," someone responds. "That was a green plastic bag and the one Lorena has is clear."

It must've been a special bag, I think. Coke wrapped up in green, the same green of money. Drugs and money always go hand in hand. Suddenly, a scream rouses us from our lethargy.

"I told you to leave me alone," the Chilena yells again. And just as quickly as she arrived, she turns to the door, gesturing to La Manuel to follow her.

"We'll be back. We're going to the bathroom," they say, closing the door behind them.

"That's right!" a *loca* scoffs. "To powder their noses, I bet."

We all laugh in unison.

"It was Junior's fault," exclaims Diva from her funeral director's seat, her voice cutting through the laughter. "That *bugarrón* was the last straw in killing her."

Silvia told me on the phone a few days ago that when Amalia was in her final days, right as she neared death's door, she somehow managed to get her boyfriend, Junior, who was in prison, to come and see her one last time. They put an electronic tag around his ankle so he couldn't escape. When he was wearing that device, they could find him wherever he went. Two police officers dropped him off, saying they'd be back to get him the next day. What happened when the two of them were alone together is irrelevant. The circumstances justified everything.

The next day, when the police showed up looking for him, no one answered the door. They had no choice but to knock it down. They found Amalia in bed, totally out of it, and Junior screaming, grabbing onto the bed so they couldn't take him away. He wanted to stay right there next to Amalia. At least she went out with a bang, I thought.

While everyone whispers, Diva de Panamá sits back down with her wide-brimmed, tea-and-milk-colored hat, in the style of a Caribbean Alexis Carrington. That's when Cristal arrives, a Central American *loca* who says she's either *Boricua* or Cuban depending on the situation, or depending on the nationality of the person supplying her party favors. She arrives carrying a tray of little plastic cups filled with clear liquid.

"Serve yourselves. I'd like to propose a toast. To Amalia, may she rest in peace. Everyone take a tequila shot." Her solemn tone lifts, and playfully, she adds, "I guess a bump would also do the trick."

47

Almost half the attendees take out a bag of coke and offer some to the person next to them. Diva calls me over.

"Hey, Monalisa, come over here and do a bump."

"Amalia was your friend . . ." I tell her.

"No. She was my sister."

We all rub our noses, gather around the casket, and take a shot. Cheers to Amalia, the Cubana!

The bump of coke leaves me feeling anxious. I want to go out for some fresh air and to drink a glass of very cold water. Slowly and without making any noise, I edge toward the exit. No one asks me where I'm going. Before I leave, I turn around. I still haven't looked the body in the face. When I do, Amalia roars with laughter. I must be hallucinating. I leave quickly, almost running. When I get outside, I sit down on the steps of the funeral home. Someone calls out my name from across the street. It's Silvia. She runs over.

"What's wrong, *loca*?"

"That bump."

"Ay, that's why I didn't want to come. It messes you up in the head." Perking up, she adds, "Let's go to the pier. We'll smoke a joint on the way to help bring you down."

We walk west. Toward the Hudson River. We smoke.

Soon we arrive at the piers. We sit on one of the benches near the water and watch as groups of adolescent *locas* arrive, all of them voguing happily, posing and strutting like models. A cool breeze tips my head back. It's getting dark. I wonder who has Amalia the Cubana's last bag of coke. I'm beginning to imagine that place they call the great beyond when someone gives my shoulder a shove. It's Silvia.

"Come on, *loca*, wake up! And let's vogue."

Jennifer's Carnations

B Y THE END of that winter night in 1997, the sidewalks outside the Senton Hotel on 27th Street between Broadway and 5th Avenue awoke covered in red carnations.

Lots of *locas* picked up tricks there. When we got to the hotel that night, after offering our services over at the Edelweiss, the pickup bar where we met contacts, we were surprised by the unusual sight of the flowers, particularly at that early hour. Eva's the one who told us. The night before, they'd found Jennifer strangled to death in one of the hotel rooms. The flowers were there for her. Most of us who went to the Edelweiss didn't know her, because she frequented another bar called Sally's, which back then was on 43rd, across from the old New York Times building.

Jennifer was a trans woman from Honduras and she was castrated. Some thought that's why she was murdered. Maybe she'd gone off with some john who thought he was with a woman, and when the time came to do the deed and he discovered he'd been fooled by a queen, he was so full of rage that he strangled her. To make matters worse, most of the guys we went off with were under the influence of some kind of narcotic. Anything could happen.

They also said she drank a lot, and that every time she got tipsy, she became totally unbearable and started insulting other *locas* and johns alike. The night of the murder, no one saw her leave the bar with a guy. They say that she was pretty drunk and that she left alone. It could have been someone who picked her up in a car or who was walking around nearby.

La Bon Bon and La Fernando saw her that night. They say she was dazzling, radiant, more beautiful than ever before. She told them it was the new hormones she was taking, a German patch that was all the rage among trans women back then. She needed to look as beautiful as possible, because she was going to Chicago to the Miss Continental pageant, and the crown would be hers. They told me that my Colombian friend La Fernando cried hysterically when she saw Jennifer in the coffin.

They say she looked like a doll inside the casket. They dressed her in a fancy blouse so no one could see the strangle marks. They cremated her the day after the wake and sent her ashes to Honduras. Apparently no one had the heart to tell her family how she'd died. All they asked was if she'd left them any money. They say Diva de Panamá took care of all the funeral expenses.

Back then, there was a party every Sunday night in a nightclub in the middle of Times Square. Everyone called it Café con Leche. The whole gay Latinx community, especially trans women, showed up. It was our night. That's where I was the first time I saw Jennifer's photograph, just a few weeks after her death. All of a sudden, they turned off the music and projected her face onto a massive screen. She was beautiful. The kind of beautiful that only a castrated trans woman in her twenties could be. As soon as they put up her photo, accompanied by the letters R.I.P., everyone stopped dancing and, chanting her name in unison, broke out into a round of applause. Without a doubt, she was now on one of the colorful clouds that awaited us in the great beyond.

We *locas* kept picking up johns in bars. Looking for tricks out on the streets. Climbing in and out of cars. No one told us to be careful or to remember what had happened to Jennifer, as though it had been something normal, almost quotidian. As Angie Xtravaganza, the mother of Xtravaganza House, said, those murders were part of what it meant to be a transsexual woman in New York. I'd add that it was part of the life of a sex worker right before the turn of the millennium and the fall of the Twin Towers. It didn't matter to anyone what happened to people like us. Jennifer didn't have a family to stand up for her. No one was keeping an eye on the detectives to see how the investigation was going, asking if they'd found any suspects. La Fernando said it well: the police weren't likely to investigate the death of yet another murdered *loca*. Even less so if she was a prostitute. Those were just the risks you ran. Only if another two or three strangled women just like Jennifer appeared would they begin to investigate, in case some psychopath was running loose.

Sometime after that, I'd say about a year, Carolina the Ecuatoriana told me she'd heard that Jennifer hadn't been killed by a john after all. That someone had wanted her dead. Apparently she'd gotten involved with the *bugarrón* of some mobster *loca*, or I should say, a *loca* with ties to the mafia because she was the manager of a hustlers' bar on 47th. Everyone knows the mafia controlled those bars back then. Jennifer, who was gorgeous and apparently started to think she was queen of the world as soon as she had four drinks in her, couldn't have cared less if the guy in question was another *loca*'s husband. Even if it was a *loca* you had to watch out for. But all that was just a conversation between some drunk queens Carolina overheard. When I brought this up with her not long ago, she told me never to mention it again. She didn't like to talk about the dead. She said they should be left in peace.

But how can Jennifer be resting in peace? It's been twenty years and they still haven't found the person responsible for her death. It's a cold case. I didn't know her, but things stay with you for a reason. Some things are destined to encircle you in a spiral of energy that transcends time and space.

A few months ago, I was sitting in my friend La Manuel's living room. After we smoked some weed, as always, she told me she had something to tell me. We'd spent the afternoon talking about the difference between the transsexuals of the past and transsexuals today. Surgery was so expensive back then that *locas* expressed themselves more through their personalities. Today it's so much easier to get surgery. In New York they'll even pay for your breast implants and facial feminization. Years ago, you had to take client after client for years to save enough money for your surgeries. Transsexuals today are pretty and that's it. Transsexuals back then weren't just beautiful, but they had strong personalities, too. They knew how to mark their territory. We got to thinking about all the *locas* we once knew who were no longer with us. All of a sudden, La Manuel stood up and went to look for something in her room. She came back with a big white envelope. She took out a photo the size of the envelope. It was of a trans girl posing nude, covering her breasts with her hands and gazing into the camera as though looking you straight in the eye.

"You won't believe it," said La Manuel, "but she was my girlfriend for a few months. She was murdered in a hotel back in '97. Her name was Jennifer."

Without saying a word, I took the photo into my hands

and thought of all my dead friends. Of Amanda, the African American trans woman with a face so many would have killed for, who was stabbed to death in the middle of Port Authority. Her murderer got out in less than seven years. I thought of the blond Colombian *loca* who looked like a Barbie who was murdered in Australia. She traveled the globe making her money.

With the photo of Jennifer still in my hands, I remembered the street full of red carnations that night. Flowers that here, in English, are called *carnations*. Just like *carne*, flesh.

Silently, I went down to the corner store. I bought a white candle and a bouquet of carnations. I set them down beside the photograph. We said a prayer for Jennifer and asked that she rest in peace.

Adriana la Chimba, or The Gorgeous Adriana de Pereira

I HAVEN'T MADE MUCH money tonight. It's time to pay rent and my wallet is beyond hungry.

"That's what you get for spending all night chatting with the *locas* instead of working," Melanie reproaches me.

"I'm just enjoying myself."

"Oh, so the *locas* are gonna pay your rent?"

"Quit nagging me. Come out with me to look for tricks."

We leave the bar and start walking along 34th Street

toward 8th Avenue. On our way, we find a mattress in the middle of the sidewalk. On 9th Avenue, to be exact, right across from where María—who's better known as the godmother of all the *maricas* in Hell's Kitchen—works.

"Come on," says Melanie. "Climb on."

"No way, are you insane? What do you want me to get on this filthy mattress for?"

"Don't say that. In Colombia, when a whore finds an abandoned mattress while she's working, she has to get onto it and jump around. It brings you money."

You can't make this stuff up.

"Well, help me, then. I can't get up with these heels on."

Melanie reaches out and gives me her hand, just like she has so many times before, just as she always does.

"Okay, hold on tight."

"*Loca*, be careful or I'll fall."

"It's your heels, *loquita*, your heels. I'm telling you, hold on tight! Now let's jump."

"Seriously? You're out of your mind, you know that?"

"I told you it won't work if we don't do it."

We hold on tight to each other and start to hop around.

"That's good, just a few more little jumps," she says, laughing uncontrollably.

"I'm so dizzy, *loca*. *No más*, please."

Back on the pavement, we balance atop our clear heels and decide to continue along our route.

"*Ay, loqui*. I hope that mattress didn't have bedbugs."

"Don't be a downer. You have to think positive or it won't work."

"I'm serious!" I retort like a kid talking back to his teacher.

"We're almost there. Let's go to my room and do a bump and then we can go back out and make ourselves a fortune."

"*Ay, sí*. Now you're talking. And all the men will be leaving for work soon. Maybe I'll find myself a nice construction worker."

"But make sure you charge him this time. You always forget to charge when you go to work horny."

"*Ay, loca*, please. That was just one time," I say, defending myself.

"Once? A few times, you mean."

We climb up the stairs in our building on 46th Street between 8th and 9th Avenues, laughing the whole way. We live on the third floor. She in one room and I in another. The building has separate units and every floor shares a bathroom. Each of us pays a thousand dollars a month. A lot of money. But, then again, we're nocturnal butterflies at the end of the twentieth century, and in the heart of Times Square, no less. I don't go into my room. Instead, we go straight to Melanie's.

"Mmm, that's more like it. I'm glad I left the AC on," she says as we walk in.

"Thank god, honey, 'cause this humidity is a bitch."

"What do you expect? It's summer. The winters here are so long, we have to take advantage."

We collapse onto the sofa. Melanie takes off her heels. I don't, because I still haven't made any money and I should go back out to make some cash.

"What're you looking at?" she says playfully. "Ah, let me guess. Something tells me you want to do a bump?"

"But of course," I tell her decisively and with a glimmer in my eye. "Don't you see I need the energy to go back out and hustle? I have to make enough for rent."

She holds out a key with coke on its point. She takes it out of a little bag she keeps inside her wig. Out from between her scalp and her blond wig, to be precise. Melanie is almost always platinum blond, but today she's more like honey blond. Blond but not too much. According to our Argentinian friend and neighbor, Francesca, who's so obsessed with Susana Giménez she seems like her clone, Melanie's been blond as long as she's known her.

"Hey, give me a little more. That was only enough for one nostril. You want me to be lopsided?"

"You're shameless," she laughs, taking another bump out of the bag with the point of her key and raising it to my nose so I can snort it.

"How lovely!" I exclaim, leaning back on the sofa.

"Careful, honey, you'll never go back out if you get too comfortable."

"Give me fifteen and then back to work, I swear."

"We'll see about that," she says, taking two ice-cold beers out of the fridge.

The one she hands me almost freezes the palm of my hand. Before we toast, Melanie pours some beer onto the floor and says, "We have to give a little to the spirits so they bring us money."

Obedient, I do the same. Ever since I dedicated myself to the life of a nocturnal urban geisha, I've become superstitious. If you're supposed to turn your back to the police station every time you walk past so you don't get locked up, I do it. If you have to spin around three times while whistling every time a black cat crosses your path, I do it. If the famous Puerto Rican astrologist Walter Mercado says putting four red roses at your door will bring you good luck, I do it. Once, while I was walking to the neighborhood flower shop after hearing in his horoscope what would bring us good weekend vibes, Melanie warned me we'd end up broke if we kept buying everything Walter Mercado told us to. We must have been spending something like two hundred bucks a month on incense, colorful ribbons, candles, and flowers, all under the expectation that it would bring us good luck. And, well, I guess it's all about faith, right?

"Cheers, babe."

"Cheers."

We sit in silence. Each one of us in our own little world. Bumps of coke can give you that side effect, I might say. That *high*, others would say. Such a high, in fact, that I don't even notice when Melanie stands up and, turning her back to me, looks out the window at the street and says, "Who could have imagined that this *loquita* would end up here. From Pereira, Colombia, all the way to New York, United States."

Sometime before this night, something in me had

learned how to be silent. My instincts know when to let someone else speak.

"My teachers were happy for me when they found out I was coming to the US. They told me I was really smart. That I could even become a doctor if I wanted to."

She pauses and turns around. She looks at me and says, "I guess you could say I do have a certain familiarity with the human body."

"Done!" I say, and we laugh. "It sounds like you had a reputation at your school for being a good student."

"Obviously I was a good student. I loved math."

"I, on the other hand, was awful with numbers. I did okay anyway, but because I studied hard, not because I liked it or because it was easy for me."

"Hand me another beer, would you, Monalisa?"

I stand up right away and take two beers out of the little fridge across from me.

"Here you go, *muñeca*."

"Thanks. And here."

She turns around with the beer in her hand and passes me a whole bag of coke. "This is for you. So you don't have to keep asking me for bumps. Now it's your turn to share with me."

I snatch it from her hands like a desperate addict. I throw myself onto the bed and offer her a bump on the point of my key. As Melanie and I always do. Then I take one myself. I stand up from the bed and lie down on the little sofa.

"Thanks again," Melanie says, propping herself up on her elbow and taking a long sip of beer.

"No problem," I reply, as though I were the one doing her a favor. That's one of Melanie's virtues, part of what makes her so humble and so loveable. She goes out of her way to do favors for other people and always ends up making it seem like they're the ones doing her a favor.

"I graduated secondary school first in my class. That was the first and only time I ever saw my father drunk. He was so proud of his son. He threw me a huge party the day I graduated."

Our silence is interrupted only by the sound of our noses sniffling.

Melanie continues.

"Honestly, I didn't like it here that much at first. But that's the way it goes, I guess. It's a *loca*'s job to send money home to her family, right?"

"You must have a bunch in savings back home," I say, trying to bring some optimism to our conversation.

"Savings? Yeah right. I've sent money home for them to save for me before, and some emergency always pops up. Your dad is sick, there's a loan to pay off, the utilities, blah, blah. I mean, I'm not complaining or anything. I'm still Adriana la Chimba, or simply," we say in unison between laughs, "the gorgeous Adriana de Pereira!"

It's not the first time I've been reminded of the name she used in her native Colombia. She's said it so many times that I and every *loca* in the bar know it by heart.

"Come on, Monalisa, give me another bump."

"Hey, I have to save something for myself," I tell her, only half in jest.

"Absolutely no shame."

I stand up. I go toward her. We each take another bump. I lie back down on the couch. For a moment, we're both quiet.

"After I turned thirteen, the money situation in my house got worse. At first I didn't pay much attention to it. But around the time I turned fifteen, I started walking the streets. I had to start hustling."

"So young?"

"That's right. I was just a *piroba*, as we say in Colombia."

A silence followed, interrupted only by the rays of light that suddenly flooded the room. A new day had begun. New York was waking up.

"What time is it?" I ask, emerging from my trance.

"Six, babe."

I sit there, pensive.

"Mmm, you don't even have to say it. Too wiped to go back out."

"Afraid so. Too many people. And it's too light outside, don't you think?"

"You're right," Melanie says. Looking me in the eye, she adds, "Hey, do you want me to lend you twenty bucks just to get you through the day? You can pay me back tonight when you work. But listen, you actually have to pay me back, I know you always play dumb."

"*Ay, loquita*, thank you. You really are too much." I realize that my friend looks exhausted. "*Muñeca*, remember to take off your makeup before you go to bed. You'll get wrinkles if you sleep with it on."

"No way, I'll never do that. I want to look pretty in my dreams, don't I?"

We laugh. I stand up to go to my room. I open Melanie's door.

"You're forgetting your twenty bucks," she reminds me, holding out a bill and giving me her hand, just as she has so many times before. Just like she always does.

Emergency Room

I T WAS AN INTENSE TIME, one of boorishness and insolence, to say it plainly. I lived alone in an apartment right in West Harlem. 139th Street between 7th and 6th Avenues. Between Lenox Avenue and Adam Clayton Powell Jr. Boulevard, to be exact. My online ads were a huge success. Manhattan is Manhattan. There's always money here.

My living room window looked out onto my building's

entrance. I could see whoever was coming to visit me perfectly.

Are you at the corner? Okay. Stay with me on the phone. Keep walking on your left side. Do you see an entrance on your left? Okay. Come up the stairs and make a right . . . And then, as soon as they turned to the right, I could see them. I never told a single one that he couldn't come up. The fact that I could see them before they saw me gave me a certain sense of security and confidence. *Keep staying on the phone and come up to the third floor.*

The door to my apartment opened directly to the stairs. I'd leave it open a crack before they made it to the third floor. *Come in and get comfortable.*

And that's how it went for a while. My friends all told me how lucky I had gotten with the apartment.

But, oh well. Nothing's perfect. Let's just say that when night comes, not even our shadows can keep us company. The johns leave. It's two or three in the morning. You're not sleepy. An inexplicable power keeps you charged up. And all of a sudden texts start rolling in from guys who want to come over. They're not clients. They're *frituras*— yes, for free—and, if you want to know the truth, each one of them is more handsome than the next. That's how people like Drew appear. He's Blatino. Half Puerto Rican, half African American. He didn't come alone. He brought with him the thing that would almost end up being my ruin: Tina Turner. I'd already had experiences with her. Sporadically. *This boy is a hustler*, I thought. He would travel to Philadelphia to make his fortune. When he came back to New York, he'd forget about his work and only wanted to party. To get high on Tina—crystal meth—in the company of a transsexual, *travesti* or "cross-dresser." And, of course, he wanted to play kinky. That's where I came in.

It wasn't that Drew was any different from my other *frituras*. He just started showing up regularly. For two months, he appeared every Saturday between four and six in the morning. What we'd do when we were high is irrelevant. What really matters is that it was with him that I started getting high on crystal meth.

Every rule has its exception, and it just so happens that he appeared once on a Thursday in the middle of the night. I was getting ready for bed when I got the text.

What's up. U up?

My heart started thumping. Not because I had a thing for him. I owed my anxiety to what was quickly beginning to seem like an addiction. Or maybe it was both. Honestly, the boy was straight out of a magazine. Or straight out of a porno, you could say, thanks to those ten inches that made him all that money in Philadelphia and that, in my experience, were entirely versatile.

Wow. Son las tres de la madrugada. *I am very tired.*

Come on. We'll have fun. We always do.

Estoy sin chavos.

Give u some money. No worries. I can give u fifty bucks.

What can I say?

I gave my subconscious a big slap in the face so it would leave me alone. And then I responded.

Come over. Ya.

I will be there in twenty minutes.

Hurry up . . .

He showed up like he always did. With that neighborhood bad-boy, pretty-boy look, with his backpack still on, like an urban gypsy. I don't remember how long he stayed. When you're high, time tends to get away from you. All of a sudden, he got up and stood next to the bed. He looked at me like he wanted more. More than what? Well, more than everything. I told him to leave. I didn't walk him to the door. He let himself out.

My mind felt stronger than my body. I was spent. It didn't matter how high I was, I fell asleep. I woke up and went straight to the fridge. I ate whatever I could find. I didn't even bother heating it up. I devoured a slice of pepperoni pizza, half a can of Coke, a doughnut. I drank milk straight from the carton, thinking it might help bring me down from my high. I lay down belly-up on the sofa. I don't know how long I stayed in that position.

I was really thirsty when I woke up. I drank water with desperation. It was cold, and the change in temperature— which felt to my Tina'd system like my body was being invaded by a stabbing pain—made me curl up in agony. I heard a voice whisper, *This is the price you pay.*

I went into the bathroom and took a long shower with lukewarm water. Under the stream of water, I planned to go out and get myself a good lunch.

I picked up the fifty-dollar bill that Drew had left me. I went to a soul food restaurant across the street. I sat down in the back. Where no one else was sitting. The waitress came over to me and, after giving me the menu, told me I had a great face.

I looked at her as if to say, *Nice try, you want me to give you a good tip.* Did I like the flattery? Obviously. I thought it must be the DNA from my mom's side, because let's just say I don't take the greatest care of myself. As my friend Silvia would put it: you're not exactly on a *caldo de pollo* diet.

I ordered southern-style fried chicken with mashed potatoes and collard greens, accompanied by a big glass of iced tea. I ate slowly, thinking it was high time I put an end to the nonstop party lifestyle. I savored every mouthful. Something inside me knew it was time to leave behind all the debauchery. Just because johns showed up offering me drugs for free didn't mean I had to take them. I lived in a great location. My ads were a success. I could make good money. I had to stop, now. I ordered an Earl Grey tea to calm my nerves and left a five-dollar tip, which the waitress thanked me for with a smile. I sorted out the day's plan in my mind and started to walk. First, to the library to borrow some DVDs to watch on my computer. I didn't have internet, so that was the best way of entertaining myself at night. I picked up a musical version of *Oliver Twist*. And the first and second seasons of *Will and Grace*. I decided to behave myself that night. I was feeling wired, so once I left the library, I walked to Washington Heights to buy some weed. I walked slowly. Enjoying the stroll. I stopped on the way to buy some Mexican avocados and whole wheat bread. For the munchies I'd get later on. As soon as he saw me, the dealer clarified that he didn't have any dime, just nickel. I thought it sounded like a great deal. I didn't even know nickels existed anymore. It must've been at least ten years since I'd last seen those little five-dollar bags. I asked for just one, because I was in savings mode.

I walked back to Harlem humming music from the eighties. I'm a vintage *loca*. An old-school queen. Once I got home, I lay down on the sofa and fell asleep.

I woke up sometime after ten at night. I posted an ad. I went to take a shower, thinking the ad would be online as soon as I came out of the bathroom. I already had the whole posting routine on autopilot, because the truth is that, after so many years in the game, I have a lot of regular clients. Guys who know me and are pleased with my services, you could say.

Just when I was ready to relax and start watching the DVDs, my phone rang. A regular. Bori-Dick. That's how I had him saved in my contacts. I'm sure you can guess why I gave him that nickname. I asked him to give me twenty minutes to get ready. While I fixed myself up, I decided this would be it for the night. No more clients.

I'd known him for almost two years, so I opened the door without even asking who it was.

"Hello. How you been?" he said. He went straight to the bed, dropped his pants, and pulled out his dick, which looked like a hanging fruit.

"Not like that, babe, we're not half-assing this. Get naked."

Before he took off his clothes, he took a glass pipe out of his backpack, along with a little bag of crack. The smoke it gives off seriously stinks, so I took a vanilla air freshener and sprayed it all over the place.

He took one hit and then another. I started sucking his cock, which began to appear in all of its glory. He blew the smoke into my face. I didn't want to inhale that smell. It's like taking a hit to the head. Smoking crack is like feeling a bunch of your neurons suddenly die.

He trembled as I sucked his dick. Deep throat. He stood on the bed with his legs open. I kneeled on the bed. He smoked and I occupied myself with a singular exercise of mouth, tongue, and throat. As he lay down again, I followed him without taking his cock out of my mouth. He started to moan softly. I knew he was about to come. I took him deep in my throat one last time and then pulled back. I watched as that thick, veiny muscle on the edge of bursting finally exploded. His stomach and my face were drenched in semen.

I stood up to get him some baby wipes and a paper towel. It wasn't enough, so I gave him more. When I say that Bori-Dick exploded, I'm not exaggerating. It exploded.

"I haven't come for a week. Work's been busy."

The corner of his mouth curled into a smile and he lit a cigarette. We gave each other a look like *up for a second round?* But then, as quickly as we looked at each other, we looked away.

"Okay, babe. Time to go," I told him.

He got dressed. He grabbed his backpack and, with his half-smoked cigarette still dangling from his lips, walked toward the door. He let himself out.

"See you later."

I went to the bathroom, and before taking off my makeup, I rinsed with mouthwash. I took off my wig and went to the living room to pass out on the couch. I remembered the nickel of marijuana. The bag was enough for a good-sized joint. I smoked half of it. I took out the computer and the DVDs I got from the library. I chose *Oliver Twist.* I lay facedown looking at the screen, waiting to see my favorite character, the Artful Dodger. More than Oliver, I wanted to see him. I imagined that in some other world, I could have been him or he could have been my best friend. I was feeling pretty chill when, suddenly, I heard a noise. *Turn on all the lights*, the voice ordered me. It was a feminine voice. Instead of hiding in my bed, I stood up and, obedient, switched on every light in my apartment. The living room light, the one in the bathroom, the one in my bedroom, and the one on the nightstand.

I went back to the bed to keep watching the movie, as though nothing had happened. But then I stood up again. This time, I picked up a plaster figurine of Our Lady of Sorrows that my friend Marylin gave me years ago. I held it up and waved it around in every corner of my room, as though the Virgin were processing.

Everything started once I put her back down on the nightstand. Something was coming. Through the door, through the windows. It felt like everything was about to explode. My pulse accelerated. My heartbeat started pounding. Boom, boom, boom. I tried to concentrate on my breathing. My focus dipped in and out, but I couldn't shake the feeling that everything was about to go under. I thought of calling 9-1-1. But I stopped myself before I made the call. I thought of the scandal that would go down if the ambulance came. And here in New York, when you call an ambulance, firemen and the police show up, too. My friend La Leo didn't deserve all that trouble. The rental contract was in her name, but since she lived in Virginia and only came to town for a few days every two weeks, we'd arranged that I could live in her apartment as long as I paid rent, and in return I'd let her stay there every time she came to New York. The apartment belonged to a low-income housing program. In short, it would be *no bueno* if they found out La Leo was subletting to someone, and even worse if they found out because I called 9-1-1.

I managed to focus on my breathing. I thought of leaving and trying to call from outside the building. At least that way the paramedics wouldn't have to come inside and I wouldn't rat out La Leo. In the end, I decided to call one of my friends. Talking with someone would help calm me down. It was after two in the morning. Everyone I knew must be awake trying to make some money. They'd be in some bar or at home posting ads, just as I'd done earlier that night. First, I called La Myriam Hernández. She didn't pick up. I called Diana. She didn't pick up. I called Pamela. She didn't pick up. I sat down on the sofa in the living room. I stood up and went to the kitchen sink. I turned on the cold water and let it run. I wet my face and drank water at the same time. While I was drying my hands, I thought of Sylvia. She wasn't putting ads up anymore and I knew she wasn't going to bars either. She was in some kind of halfway house.

"What's going on?" I heard from the other end of the line.

I could tell from her tone of voice that she'd been cozy in her bed with the air-conditioning on full blast.

"*Ay*, honey. I've taken so many things in the last few days that I think I'm having some kind of panic attack."

"Well, try having a beer or something to see if it'll calm you down," she said with complete calm, making me realize she must have been through the same thing many times before.

"I don't have any beer. You know I don't drink."

"Hmm . . . you don't drink, but . . ."

She managed to get a smile out of me.

"Hey, I feel a little better now, but can we keep talking until this awful feeling goes away?"

"*Uy*, the same thing happened to me years ago," Silvia said. "Someone put some kind of pill in my drink without me seeing it. I couldn't remember anything the next day. They told me I even wrecked a cop's clothes. It's a miracle I didn't end up in jail."

"That's terrible," I said, a bit more at ease. Talking with someone made me feel better. I was much more relaxed.

"What are you even doing up?" Silvia asked when she realized what time it was.

"Putting up ads. Trying to make some money."

"I hear you."

And as soon as Silvia said this, I started to hear a kind of continuous whistle.

"*Oye*, I can't hear you very well. There's some kind of whistle."

"I can hear you perfectly."

"It must be your phone or mine. I'm hanging up, I'll call you right back."

Then I heard the whistle sounding loudly in the space around me, and everything that had relaxed me up to that point suddenly transformed into sheer panic. It wasn't a problem with my phone. The whistle continued, as if heralding a catastrophe.

I tried breathing deeply again. I tried to concentrate. With my cell phone, I called Sylvia's number again.

"Sylvia, stay on the line. I'm going to the emergency room at Harlem Hospital. I think something's happening to me."

Without putting down the phone, I started to get dressed very slowly. I put on some shoes, pants, and a T-shirt. I also put on a baseball cap that said *NY.* I picked up the keys and opened the door. Thankfully, the stairs and all the hallways of the building were well lit. I set off, describing every single thing I did to Sylvia.

"I'm dead bolting the door. Now I'm starting to go down the stairs. I'm on the third floor. I'm leaving my building. I'm walking. It's almost 4:00 A.M., everything here is quiet and dark, Sylvia. Stay there. Just two more blocks to Harlem Hospital. Please don't hang up. Just stay with me. Let's just talk about whatever."

I didn't say anything else. I just listened to Sylvia as she spoke to me. I have no idea about what. I was so terrified, I was convinced that at any moment, something might jump out of one of the parked cars or trees that lined the street. Finally, I got to Lenox Avenue. The hospital was all lit up before me. It was like an oasis in the middle of the desert I was trying to reach. Before something bad happened to me. Before something trapped and devoured me.

How long did it take me to cross the street? I don't remember. I only know it took much longer than usual. I managed to reach the doors of the hospital. The entrance to the emergency room. A guard saw my panicked expression and opened the door for me.

"Are you okay?"

"So, so," I replied.

I went into the waiting room. I sat down and started to relax a bit. I could hear Sylvia on the other end of the line asking me if I'd made it.

"Yes, Sylvia, thank you. I don't know what I would've done without you."

That's when she started yelling at me—calling me out, really—asking when was I going to learn my lesson, when was I going to stop filling my body with all that trash. I thanked her again and then hung up on her.

I had to wait to be seen by a nurse. I was anxious. At that hour, the hospital was basically empty. I stood up and walked over to the security guards. They were both African American. A man and a woman in their thirties. Both of them had big brown eyes.

"*Uf*, I'm feeling better. I was sort of paranoid before."

"What happened?" the woman asked.

"I heard a voice. Then I think I had a panic attack."

They both started to laugh at me.

"Why's that?"

Again, it was the woman who spoke.

"I've been partying a lot. You know, taking lots of stuff."

I heard someone call my name. The nurse was ready to see me. The first thing she did was ask me why I was there. I told her the same thing I told the couple. That I'd heard a voice telling me to turn on all the lights. And then I had the anxiety attack. She sat there looking at me and taking notes on a piece of paper. She took my pulse. She asked me to go back to the waiting room.

I sat down close to a window facing the street. The sun was already coming up. It was calm outside. Little by little, I started to feel better. I stood up and went back to where the nurse had examined me.

"You know what? I feel better now. I'm really relaxed. Thanks so much, but I think I'm going home. I just live two blocks away. I think I just need to sleep it off. Thanks again. I'm headed out."

Before I could take a step, she asked me to wait for just a minute. She said it wouldn't hurt for me to see a doctor first. That I'd only have to wait three minutes. I went back to the same place where I'd been sitting. I waited. I started to concentrate on my breathing. Once again, I stood up and went over to the nurse.

"Seriously, I'm much better now. I'm just super tired. Thanks anyway, but I'm going to head out."

I hadn't finished saying this when a Mexican man approached me who, judging by his uniform and the stethoscope hanging from his neck, I guessed was a doctor or a nurse.

"I was just telling the young lady I feel better. I'd really just prefer to go home. I only live two blocks from here."

A police officer arrived and positioned himself at my side. His body language seemed to indicate that I shouldn't move, that they weren't going to let me leave.

"Let's go," said the Mexican doctor.

And I, obedient as ever, followed him, escorted by two people in uniform: one in light blue and the other in navy. We walked down a long hall. We passed a section they were remodeling. Then we arrived at an elevator I could tell wasn't for public use. I rode up with my companions. I'd say we stopped between the fifteenth and twentieth floors, but I never saw the numbers. It seemed to go straight up. As soon as I set foot outside the elevator, I saw a guard in front of me. He asked me to hand over all my belongings. The first things I gave him were my keys and my cell phone. I couldn't understand what was going on. I entered a room and a door closed behind me with a sound like a metallic crypt shutting. High up on the wall, I read PSYCHIATRIC UNIT. Another guard appeared and asked me to take off my shoes and give them to him. This is worse than a police station, I thought. All you have to do there is take your shoelaces off in case the spirit moves you to strangle yourself or someone else. Later I learned that some patients try to hit people with their shoes. Once I was barefoot, I crossed through another metal door that shut behind me, heavy and abrupt just like the first one.

The room I was in had an immaculate hardwood floor. Like the floor in a school run by nuns. It was a rectangular space with a clear circular booth in the middle, where the hospital personnel sat. From there, they watched us.

It was very early. Maybe six in the morning. I sat down on a kind of bench attached to the wall. Across from me, on another bench, a guy was sleeping. I couldn't see his face. Just his head of purple hair. Next to me, another man was sleeping on a cot with one hand handcuffed to the wall. I realized that all around the wall, in addition to the seating, there was a long metal bar like they have in ballet schools, to which two other men were handcuffed.

I didn't like this place at all. That's when someone called my name. A woman appeared in a window of the clear central booth. I stood up and went over to her.

"You have to wait until the doctors get here at eight thirty," she snapped without even looking me in the eye.

"What time is it now?" I asked.

"Seven A.M. Please take a seat and wait for them to call you, sir."

I went back. Another barefooted guy appeared in front of me. None of us had shoes on. He was trotting around the room. He held his right hand up in the air like he was running the final meters of a marathon. He ran around and around the observation booth in circles.

Suddenly a woman in a hospital uniform arrived carrying a trayful of sandwiches. I was so anxious I could have eaten the whole tray. I took one tuna and one egg salad. I asked if there was coffee, and immediately, another woman in uniform appeared carrying a tray of drinks. I took a cup of coffee and an orange juice. At least the service was good.

The two women in uniform disappeared into the

booth. The trays they were carrying were still full. I was the only person who'd taken something. Marathon man didn't stop running. You could hear a kind of echo emanating from his throat. I devoured the sandwiches. I went over to the little window to ask for more coffee. They told me the women with the trays would be back in forty-five minutes.

I went back to my spot. I looked through the barred windows. It was a very tall tower. Someone turned on a television built into the wall. *Good Morning America* was the program they were going to force me to watch. I watched carefully, thinking this might make the time fly by. Before they even gave the weather report, I heard my name.

They opened a door and asked me to walk into the room. In front of me stood a tall white woman in a medical uniform. A psychiatrist, no doubt. She made me go into a small room. She offered me a seat, and before she'd even asked me anything, I blurted out my entire recent history of drug consumption leading up to the moment I heard the voice. The doctor paid special attention when I told her about going to Washington Heights to buy marijuana. She asked me to repeat that part. She took notes. She made me go out and wait outside for a few minutes while she consulted with her colleagues.

As soon as I walked out of the room, I realized the two women with the trays were about to leave. I ran after them. I took two sandwiches again, one tuna and one egg salad, as well as coffee and orange juice.

I went back to my spot. I noticed there was a new visitor, a woman sitting very close to me. She told me between sobs that she didn't understand why they'd brought her to that place. Then a nurse came over and asked her if she'd taken her meds. The woman said she didn't like all the pills. There were just too many of them. The nurse went away and the woman kept crying. The nurse returned with a small silver tray that held a glass of water and pills of different sizes and colors.

"Take them," she commanded.

Less than five minutes later, when the woman had stopped crying and was sleeping deeply, two men in white lab coats appeared and loaded her onto a gurney. They carried her away, disappearing behind a door that, unlike all the others, was not transparent but instead made of metal.

The man with purple hair sleeping across from me

woke up. He started to sit up slowly, stretching out his arms. His face was swollen from so much sleeping. His fat face, and especially his dyed purple hair, reminded me of Ursula, the villain from *The Little Mermaid*, and I just had to laugh at the whole scene. Marathon man was gone. They must have taken him away, too. One of the guys who was handcuffed to the metal bar woke up and shouted. The same uniformed men who had taken the woman appeared, carrying him off on the gurney as he screamed for help.

I started to get nervous. I went up to the window again.

"Miss, I've been here for hours. Everyone who was here before me left already. I spoke with the doctor and I honestly feel good now. Please just tell me how long until I can leave."

I said this as calmly as possible. I knew if I wasn't careful with everything I said and did, it could be used against me later on. For the first time, she looked me straight in the eye and answered.

"The doctors are discussing whether to release you or not."

I stood there like a deer in headlights. The women with the trays arrived again, but I was so terrified by the possibility that they'd keep me locked up in that place, or that they'd take me to the psych ward at Bellevue, that I lost my appetite. Almost as though they knew what was happening to me, the women left two little sandwiches next to my seat, one tuna and one egg salad, along with coffee and orange juice. The woman's response echoed in my mind.

People came and went, all of them behaving strangely. Men and women in uniform appeared and disappeared through the metal door. I heard my name again. I went into the booth and then into the room where the psychiatrist had interviewed me. She was sitting. She offered me a chair. We sat face to face.

"What my colleagues and I were concerned about is that you mentioned hearing voices. That's why we didn't know whether to let you go or not, but when you told us about the marijuana you bought on the street, we understood your situation a little better. We've seen several recent cases of people buying cheap marijuana off the street and ending up in the emergency room of some New York hospital with a panic attack. It seems like they're using some kind of spray on the marijuana to make its effects more potent. We're not sure, but we think it could be angel dust. That spray sells like hotcakes. We recommend you don't buy any more marijuana off the street, and you should also look into a Narcotics Anonymous program. You are free to go."

The only thing I could think of to say was thank you.

In less than twenty minutes, I was out. In the street. Walking the two blocks in the shadow of the same trees that had frightened me so much the night before. I carried my shoes in my hands. I went straight to bed to sleep all the hours I hadn't slept, and while I walked, I thought about the grave mistake the doctors had made when, once again, they let me go.

Biuty Queen

THE TRUTH IS THAT, YES, I'm exhausted. But it was worth all the hustling, all the johns. All those fucking clients so I could afford to have my dresses made, on top of paying the choreographer and the four dancers. Obviously, it was worth it. The crown looks gorgeous on me. It might not have so many jewels, but you can tell it was expensive. Mirror, mirror on the wall, who's the sluttiest New York *loca* of them all? Go ahead, say it. Speak up, I can't hear

you. Better you say it than me. Yes, exactly. Deborah
Hilton. Deborah with an *H*. Yours truly. José Troncoso
doesn't exist anymore. We left him thousands of kilo-
meters behind.

Look. If you'd taken any longer to say my name, who
knows what I would've done to you. You got lucky; I was
about to get suspicious and learn the hard way that
breaking a mirror brings you seven years' bad luck. You
guessed it, honey: the slut is me. Deborah Hilton. Deborah
with an *H*. I have five crowns. And a ticket to Chicago
for next year. To the most important beauty pageant for
transsexuals in all the United States. I mean, no one wins
that crown the first time. Jim Flint, the founder and orga-
nizer, makes sure you go at least three times before you
win. And that's just if you're beautiful, talented, and on
top of it all, you spend a fortune on the production. I think
the only person who's ever won the crown her first time is
Lady Kathiria. First she won the Continental Plus title.
That's the one for chubby girls. You'll notice I didn't say
fat. Then the *loca* slimmed down and went back for the
Continental Regular the next year. She won first place.
You have to give the queen some credit. They say she was
buried with all her crowns. Hey, don't give me that look. I

was just thinking about how many crowns I'll have before I cross over to the other side. *Uy*, best not to think about that. I'm going to have a drink. Oh, right, you don't drink. You're a mirror. An object. I like you anyway. Cheers. And keep reflecting my gorgeousness. Just remember: I'm not like everyone else. I talk to you. I tell you all my secrets.

After Miss Continental, I'm going to Miss International Queen in Thailand. Sure, I'll have to invest more in surgeries, because obviously the most beautiful *locas* in the whole world will be there. And you can't forget that Asian girls already have the figure, the skin, and the hair going for them. Feminine perfection. But anyway, that's two years away. Although two years is nothing here in New York. After all, it's been more than ten since I came here from Central America and it feels like it was just yesterday.

So, for now, my job is to focus on next September and getting ready for Chicago. I'll have to raise at least $20,000. *Pero* first things first, I need to pay off my debts *ahora mismo* because my landlord's about to take me to court. I owe more than three months' rent. By some miracle, God gave me plenty of beauty and plenty of dick. I'll never have a shortage of clients, and with the regulars

I already have from nonstop hustling, I'll be caught up in a month. That deserves another toast. Duh, to keep my spirits up. Cheers, mirror. Thanks for listening.

Now that I think about it, maybe beginning in November I'll start to travel and look for tricks in places outside the city. Monday to Thursday in Long Island or Jersey, and Fridays and weekends in Manhattan, obviously, because money never runs out here. But if we're being honest, the competition gets stiffer every day. Outside the city, it's a different story. There aren't even bars for *locas*. There might be for gays, but not for beauties like us. We can charge whatever we want out there. Of course, you have to be extra careful about the police. If they see men coming and going from your room, the hotel always calls the cops. And the *loca*? Straight to the slammer she goes. It's good I have my permanent residence, but I still have to watch out. Remember what happened to the Torres family—even people with papers can get deported. And that, my dear little mirror, is simply not my cup of tea. I have crowns left to win. I want to have so many they don't even fit in my casket. I hope I need a second coffin just for my crowns. Don't judge me just because I'm drunk. Look, I'll make sure they bury you with me, too. Will I live to be an old lady? If I do, whoever goes to my wake is going to see a photo exhibition of me posing with all my crowns. *Look at that old* maricón, they'll say, *who'd ever believe he was a biuty queen?* Yes, *mi amor*, a lady must do everything she can to be respected.

But let me tell you something. All those dancers and choreographers are bloodsuckers. They charge for everything. Zero solidarity. Even knowing how we kill ourselves working. La Ángel just went to a pageant in Miami and rented a van to save on the plane tickets. She was planning to take the makeup artist and two *locas* who'd be her assistants, but they did squat for her in the end. Took off as soon as they got to the pageant. Didn't even thank her. Anyway, these *maricas* said they weren't about to spend that many hours sitting in a van, they'd only fly. If not, she'd have to look for some other dancers. And what could the *loca* do? Well, nothing. She had to suck it up and ask me to borrow some money. La Ángel ended up spending just as much on the tickets for the four dancers and the choreographer as she did on her evening gown. Of course I lent her the money. She's my friend. Such a good friend that she still owes me half of it. I'm going to call her first thing tomorrow morning so she pays me. That's how a girl ends up broke. Still gorgeous, though. Not just anyone can say she won crowns for beauty pageants in New York. I can. Deborah Hilton. Deborah with an *H*. Okay, one last toast. *Uy*, who's calling at this hour? And when I'm so exhausted. Oh! It's Anthony. The client with the deep pockets. I'll wait five minutes and then call him back. He likes when you play hard to get. This boy sucks up drugs like a vacuum. I'll make a whole month's rent off him alone. Tomorrow my landlord will be happy. And if I get more out of him than I think, the extra will go straight into my piggy bank for Chicago. Okay, it's time. I'm calling him. *Pero* please don't get mad at me for moving you from your spot. You know I keep my drugs between your back and the wall. Tomorrow I'll tell you how it went. And you know what? I'm going to leave my crown on, just like the biuty queen I am.

Little Miss Lightning Bolt

〜❀〜

I'VE BEEN SLEEPING FOR AGES. One *that's enough* gives me the push I need to get out of bed. Rise and shine. I pick up my phone and look over my missed calls. A bunch of them are from La Manuel. I don't want to talk with her. I'm done being lectured. Sometimes I'd rather just ignore the calls. I have a few from unsaved numbers and one from someone named Claudia. I rack my brain. Claudia? Oh, La Rayito! I call her right away. She picks up on the third ring.

"Who is it?"

"It's me, Monalisa. I had a missed call from you."

"Oh, yeah! What's up, Mona? I was thinking of heading over to Washington Heights to buy some weed."

"Let's meet at 175th and Broadway. We can find some there. Remember I live in the Bronx now, but right by the bridge, so it's basically the same thing. Can we say seven thirty? I just woke up. I need a little time."

"Well, hurry up, queen!" she says from the other end of the line.

I haven't left the Bronx in three days. It's been two weeks since I got fired. Unemployed, yet again. For days I've been self-medicating with sex and narcotics. It's time I crossed the bridge. The one that takes you from 181st and University Avenue in the Bronx over to 181st and Amsterdam Avenue in Manhattan.

I take a long, hot shower. I shave and admire my gorgeous skin, still radiant and soft after a half century of nonstop tango. As soon as I return to my room, I look in the top drawer of my nightstand for a hormone patch. I have three left. I stick one on my left arm close to my shoulder. The same spot where they give you a vaccine. Before I get dressed, I touch and play with my nipples, which are pink and erect from the effect of the hormones. I make sure my socks and underwear are clean. I need to bundle up. This has been one of the longest and hardest winters. It's seven thirty. I'm right on time for my meeting with La Rayito. I don't want to take the bus. I'd rather walk across the bridge. It's Sunday. The frigid wind that fills the space between the bridge and the dark waters of the East River makes the skin on my face feel taut. Nothing like the cold to tighten up the flesh. Day turns to night as I walk. Bicycles whiz by in both directions, their coming and going keeping me alert. I feel like I'm turning into the figure from Munch's *The Scream*. Luckily, I make it across before this happens. I'm on 181st and Amsterdam. The neighborhood's still humming. I like walking down these streets. It fills me with just the kind of energy I need these days. When I reach 175th Street, I turn to my right to get to Broadway. Not even five minutes have passed when I see La Rayito coming. I hold up my hand and start to wave. As soon as she sees me, she does the same.

"Monalisa!" she calls. We give each other a kiss on each cheek.

"Let's go get the weed. We can smoke and walk that

way," I propose with all the authority I deserve after having lived in this neighborhood for years.

"Sounds divine. So many handsome *bugarrones* around here."

"This neighborhood is full of good-looking *tígueres*," I reply as we walk the two blocks to where we'll buy the weed.

We complete our transaction and start to walk, casually wandering around to make ourselves less visible. Like a kind of shield. A kind of protection.

"*Ay, loca*. It's not like I don't have energy, but you're leaving me in the dust. How do you never get tired of walking? Unless I tell you to stop, you just keep on going. Now I get why they call you La Rayito."

"That's right, queen. They named me Rayito because I could knock out the other guys like a lightning bolt."

"What do you mean?"

"When I was fifteen, I competed in street fights. That's how I made money."

"Hey, I think that marijuana's hitting you a little hard. You're trying to tell me you were a boxer?" I say, incredulous, as I take a long hit.

"Yes, *loca*, did you think I was pulling your hair?"

"What hair, honey? Can't you see I'm bald?"

We laugh and stop smoking. We're already pretty far gone.

"When I was just a *chavito*, the guys in my neighborhood always picked on me. I dealt with it, but a time came when I said enough is enough. After that, if anyone laid a finger on me, I'd knock him out cold. Then, when I was older, I found out my dad had been paying those guys to pick on me."

It's winter, but the sky is clear. The moon is full, its light the light of memory.

"Let's walk," I say. "We'll look for some nice eye candy. It's almost time for the bad boys to come out."

"Let's do it," says La Rayito, sitting up in a flash and beginning to walk.

"Hey, Little Miss Lightning Bolt. Walk, don't run. You know I don't have your energy."

We walk through the neighborhood, our eyes savoring the sight of those gorgeous *tígueres*. I imagine La Rayito in some corner of Guadalajara exchanging punches with some guys.

"My dad knew exactly what he was doing. He organized underground fights. My neighborhood was number fifty-four. Every neighborhood had a number. They were all slums on the outskirts of Guadalajara. My dad became a kind of manager for me, I guess."

"And you made money?"

"Of course. I could make up to five thousand pesos in a single weekend. I'd end up pretty beaten up, but at least my pockets were full of cash."

"Yeah, I know, we *locas* are tough. A whore on San Camilo Street in Santiago once told me a queen is like a rubber ball. They can throw us out of moving cars, but we just bounce right back up to our feet and keep on walking."

We stop by a bakery to buy coffee. We pick up some cheese empanadas while we're at it, and then we keep walking around.

"Even though I was giving all my money to my family, I still managed to save up enough to go to Tijuana in less than a year. From there I paid a coyote to help me cross the border. Getting across is a complete nightmare. I can't even do it justice. You have to leave people along the way, and before you know it, they're a little snack for the vultures. You know it and you see it. You lose your sense of time. You lose track of the days you've been walking through the desert."

"And here you are, Miss Lightning Bolt. Here you are."

"That's right. Here we are, Monalisa, just strolling through Washington Heights, rather fumigated on weed."

"Fumigated like cockroaches."

"That was all so long ago. The only thing left is my name. Lightning Bolt."

All of a sudden, she pauses. A tall, dark guy stops to talk to her. Grinning, she tells me she'll be right back and asks me to wait for her.

I watch as she sets off with her new companion. I know they aren't coming back. I start my journey back to the Bronx. It's after 10:30 P.M. As soon as I step onto the bridge, cold invades my whole body until, all of a sudden, it gives way to a kind of heat. Little Miss Lightning Bolt will knock out any violent spirit that crosses my path. I feel safe. I walk across the icy bridge back to the Bronx, accompanied by the strength of my Mexican friend. And the strength of so many others who know what it means to cross from one side to the other, what it means to get home in one piece, full of memories and without a trace of bitterness.

The Boricua's Blunts

I MET EL BORI A FEW TIMES. La Manuel said the boy went up to her one day while she was walking through Port Authority close to the shelter. He asked if she'd take him home with her, saying she shouldn't be frightened, he wasn't going to rob her or anything, he was a good guy. Of course my friend said yes.

This was right before the blackout of 2003, before all of New York lost power. I'd never seen my friend like that, so head over heels in love. When I got to her studio that afternoon, I asked her to tell me all about him. La Manuel told me to wait. Willie had just gone out for a Pepsi. Soon I'd see him with my very own eyes.

I'd just started opening a box of Dunkin' Donuts to present to La Manuel, to make it clear I was pitching in with snacks for when we got the munchies, when the door opened, and who walked in but a white, twenty-something Boricua with clear, sky-blue eyes.

"This is my friend," La Manuel told him in the way of an introduction. Typical. You know how well-known we Latinos are here for our good manners.

"What's up," Willie greeted me. His whole bad-boy act didn't seem to match his good-guy expression or his relaxed-guy vibe.

As I said hi, I thought about how good the boy looked, but I knew he belonged to my friend. *O sea*, untouchable. He wasn't Willie anymore; I decided right then and there to call him the Boricua or El Bori. El Bori passed the bottle of Pepsi and a pack of Marlboro Light 100s to La Manuel. She took out a cigarette and gave the pack back to him. It looked like they were passing a ball back and forth in a baseball game. La Manuel has definitely mastered this guy's body language.

El Bori put a cigarette between his lips and searched in his right pants pocket for some cash to give La Manuel. She gave me a look like, *"Mira, chulita,* he brought back change."* I looked at her with a desperate expression that said, *"Ya, pues,* let's get going with the weed." La Manuel heard me loud and clear. She took out a bag of weed and tossed it to El Bori, followed by a blunt. They kept up their routine of two baseball players tossing a ball back and forth.

"Vamos, roll one up," she ordered El Bori, who started to empty the blunt and fill it with marijuana. He used up the whole bag. If it's up to me, because I'm old school, I prefer to roll blunts with bamboo paper.

We got high. La Manuel and I talked about everything and nothing. We each asked the other about our friend Sylvia. That morning, we'd both spoken to her on the phone.

El Bori stayed there, at our side, sitting on a corner of the bed. He looked absent, like he was somewhere else.

"What's up with him?" I asked La Manuel as quietly as I could. She shrugged as if to say she had no idea.

All of a sudden, she jumped out of the only chair in the studio, where she'd been sitting oh so comfortably.

"Time for our munchies! Here we have some doughnuts

the *loqui* brought, and with this Pepsi, we're all set," she announced.

La Manuel opened the Dunkin' Donuts box with great ceremony and offered them to us.

"You might as well take two or three now. I know you," she teased me.

I took three. Two of my favorite, Boston cream, and another filled with strawberry jelly. Before I started to devour them, I stood up to pour the Pepsi into cups full of ice. The three of us sat in silence again. El Bori looked even more absent than before.

"Let's go out!" I said, suddenly springing to my feet. La Manuel followed suit. We went down the stairs of the old building. El Bori trailed behind.

These were my first memories of the Boricua. Sometime after that, I lost touch with La Manuel. Too much drama about drugs and money, if I'm being honest. Years passed and we didn't see each other. Until one day, while walking through Times Square, I ran into El Bori. I recognized him immediately. He looked like a grown man. He must have been close to thirty years old. We said hi to each other. I asked him if he still saw La Manuel. He said yes, she was pretty sick, she'd been diagnosed with colon cancer.

This should have produced anguish or despair in me, but the truth is that, in our circle, fatal illnesses are pretty run of the mill. The only thing that occurred to me was to ask if she was okay. He said she was following the treatment and that he was taking care of her himself.

We exchanged numbers. We promised to call each other that night. I really wanted to speak with La Manuel, but my wish wouldn't come true. I lost the piece of paper where I'd written down the number.

A few years later, which in New York is the blink of an eye, I was on an R train going to Astoria, Queens, when, around four stops before my destination, I saw someone with a familiar face get in and sit down across from me. It was her, La Manuel. We looked at each other and, without even saying a word, stood up to give each other a big hug.

We agreed that neither of us had changed a bit. Neither of us did drugs anymore. Correction: we didn't do as many as we used to. We swapped phone numbers. I had a cell phone by then, so I saved it right away so I wouldn't have to worry about losing it again. La Manuel lived in Harlem and I was living in Washington Heights. We were close by. After that chance encounter, we started to see each other frequently.

One of those nights when I went to see La Manuel, she told me El Bori was coming to stay with her for a few days. They weren't together anymore, but they'd become close friends. She said El Bori had been good to her while she was sick. That he'd even had to clean her more than once.

He arrived one night in the middle of winter. La Manuel called me right away to invite me over to eat; she'd cooked *arroz moro* and chicken breasts to welcome him. You don't have to tell me twice. I flew there.

As soon as I entered my friend's apartment, I greeted El Boricua affectionately, but he didn't answer. I said hi to him again, thinking he hadn't heard me, and still he said nothing. La Manuel shot me a look that said I shouldn't take it personally. I should let it go. We'd better just eat.

"*Mmm. Qué delicioso.* I'll do the dishes," I said as soon as I'd scarfed down the last bite. I wanted to show my gratitude for the succulent feast.

"*Ay, no*," said La Manuel. "This isn't the first time you've offered. And no offense, but you always leave them sort of dirty. Let's just roll ourselves a blunt and I'll make us some coffee."

"All right, but you can't say I didn't offer."

As always, La Manuel tossed a bag of weed and a blunt over to El Bori. He took apart the blunt to put the weed in while my friend, in the kitchen, hummed a song.

Once El Bori finished rolling, he stood up as though he'd only just seen me and gave me an enthusiastic hug.

"Hey, it's so great to see you."

"Yeah, you too," I answered with the same enthusiasm, not knowing if he was joking or being serious.

La Manuel, refined as ever, came out of the kitchen carrying three cups of coffee on a silver platter. And while she deposited everything on the center table, she whispered to me not to say anything. We sat down to have a coffee and to smoke the blunt. Soon El Bori started talking. He wasn't addressing La Manuel or me. He was speaking to someone else. We were high. I didn't pay him any mind. I started chatting with La Manuel about one of our favorite conversation topics: trans beauty pageants. We got all wrapped up in an argument over who was the most beautiful winner of Miss Continental, the most prestigious pageant, which was held every year in Chicago over Labor Day. She said it was Mimi Marks. I argued that Erika Andrews hadn't just been one of the most beautiful winners, but also one of the most talented. Then we sat in silence, tired after all that clucking like Swarovski crystal parrots. El Bori didn't stop communicating with himself.

He stayed at La Manuel's place for another week or so before he went back to Chicago. A job was waiting for him there. And, it appeared, a girlfriend, too. I didn't ask La Manuel about El Bori's strange behavior. I understood without her even saying it that she preferred it that way.

On another one of El Bori's visits a few months later, La Manuel called to ask me if I'd bring over a *flan* from Washington Heights. A few days before that, I'd gone to see them, and El Bori hadn't left the bedroom the whole afternoon. La Manuel said it was so that he wouldn't hear voices. I wanted to impress them, so I bought one egg *flan* and one coconut. When I arrived and delivered them ceremoniously, she said to me, as she always did:

"*Gracias, loqui.* You shouldn't have. I'm going to save them for tonight, I lost my craving. All I want to do right now is sleep. Also, I took half a Percocet."

My friend was basically a pharmacy on legs.

"Sit down in the living room and watch some TV. I'm going to lie down. There's soda in the fridge."

"What about El Bori?"

"He went to the store for a blunt. But I'm not going to

smoke. That pill already did me in. You should smoke with him."

"Okay," I said, arranging myself on the red leather sofa and putting on CNN *en Español*.

"All right. Let me know before you leave," she said, disappearing behind the bedroom door.

I sat there, surprised, watching television. They'd eliminated DACA, the policy that protected thousands of children who were brought to this country by their parents, that helped them become documented. Trump is an imbecile, a pig. I was talking to myself when the apartment door opened and El Bori greeted me.

"Hi," I said, shocked. I was positive he wasn't going to pay attention to me.

"Let's smoke," he proposed, holding up a blunt and a bag of weed.

He rolled the blunt in record time. I watched him with pleasure, thinking about how good he looked. We smoked and hummed a Frankie Ruiz song that goes, "*la cura resulta más mala que la enfermedad.*" I didn't want to keep watching the news; that little shit Trump reminded me of Pinochet. I turned off the television to focus on El Bori, on the soft crooning of songs I've heard so many times from other Boricua friends. We were rather stoned. We looked at each other. Our eyes were red like rabbits'. We laughed.

"Let's go out," said El Bori, standing.

"Super."

I stood right up and we left without saying anything to La Manuel. We let her sleep.

"Let's go to Washington Heights. I'm gonna buy some weed, *papi* ran out."

It's so sweet he calls La Manuel *papi* I thought, looking at him with tenderness.

We stopped by the liquor store. We bought ourselves some little bottles of booze, one for each of us. It was cold, and we had a long walk ahead of us. We each took a sip as soon as we left the store. It was 3:30 P.M. on a Thursday in February. In another hour it would start to get dark. We walked along 132nd Street toward 5th Avenue. We walked to 135th and continued west from there. Then along St. Nicholas all the way to 175th.

El Bori sang as he smoked a Marlboro Light 100. We stopped right before we got to 145th and Amsterdam. We stood in the space formed by the facades of those houses from the twenties, the ones where you have to walk up four steps to get to the front door. They fill up with rats at night. We took a drink. We each had half a bottle left. El Bori looked at me.

"*Oye*, I've wanted to ask you something for a while now."

"Shoot."

"What was your childhood like in Chile?"

I didn't know how to answer. Hundreds of images came to mind. And I felt pleasure at having lived through everything I've lived. I gave him my answer in the form of a smile.

El Bori looked at me, smiled along with me, and said it seemed like a happy time.

We started walking again and turned onto St. Nicholas going uptown. Thirty more blocks and we'd be in the middle of Washington Heights. A cold, icy wind blasted us. We turned our backs to it. We hopped up and down so we wouldn't freeze. El Bori said the wind in Chicago was even worse. We drank what remained in our makeshift canteens and continued on toward the heights of Manhattan. As we walked, Dominican bakeries started to appear, multicolored *bizcochos* adorning their window displays. I went into one of them, making the excuse that it was new and I wanted to see what it was like inside. I treated him to a *morir soñando* and I had a coffee accompanied by a slice of coconut and pineapple cake. El Bori slurped up every last drop of the *morir soñando.*

It couldn't have been later than five when we got to Washington Heights, but it was already dark out. We went straight to get the weed. When choosing between all the spots I know, I picked the one with the best-looking *tígueres.* El Bori took out a twenty-dollar bill and passed it to me. He said it would be better if I bought it because they didn't know him. I told him no worries, he was with me and he wouldn't look much different from any other *tipo* from the hood. He gave me a sideways glance like he didn't appreciate my comment. The boys were somewhere between eighteen and twenty years old. There were a few guys riding back and forth on bikes. They had to be the ones who kept a lookout for the cops. The *tígueres* looked El Bori up and down, trying to figure out his background. They could tell he was Boricua. There's a rivalry between Dominicans and Boricuas I've never understood. We stopped in front of one of them. El Bori passed him the twenty-dollar bill with attitude. With the very same attitude, the dealer gave him the bag of weed.

We went to the park to roll a blunt and smoke looking at the Washington Bridge. On the way, we saw a bunch of teenagers leaving the high school across from the park. They were the children of Latino immigrants, born here. The children of Dominicans, Mexicans, and here and there, a child of Asian immigrants, too. Most likely Chinese.

El Bori rolled one quickly, in case a cop was around. We saw the Washington Bridge in all of its glory. It looked impressive all lit up like that. We saw the traffic piling up between New York and New Jersey.

We smoked and sat on the benches, turning our backs to the river and the view. It was dark. The sound of cars and people coming and going served as a reminder that the city still wasn't sleeping.

"Let's go," I told him, coming out of my daze. "I'll show you how to get back."

We left the park. We walked to 168th along Fort Tryon Avenue. When we got to Broadway, we started walking downtown.

When we reached the slab of concrete that is New York Presbyterian, just a few blocks from my house, I decided to part ways with El Bori. The fatigue had gotten to me and I told him so. The street was well lit. I could see his sky-blue eyes. They were crystalline. He held out his hand to say goodbye. As I gave him my hand, I saw a tattoo on his.

"Is that new?"

"No. I've had it for years."

"What is it? It looks like a name or something."

"Yeah, it's my mom's. See you around."

"Tell La Manuel I'll call her."

About three days later, I got a text from La Manuel. *Call me.* She told me El Bori had gone back to Chicago two days ago. That morning, they'd called to ask if she was a relative. Her phone number was all they'd found in El Bori's records. Yes, I'm his uncle, La Manuel had told them. It was a doctor. They were calling to say that El Bori had been admitted to a psychiatric ward. La Manuel hadn't been able to talk with him, but they gave her the number for the people who were caring for him. He wouldn't be leaving for a while, they told her. He was under observation.

I told my friend I'd be right over. She'd run out of weed and asked me to bring some. I knew it was more necessary than ever. When I arrived, she was pensive. In the living room, we rolled a joint in my old-school way. With bamboo paper. We smoked slowly.

"El Bori was just a kid. He must've been eight or ten. I think he was ten, yeah, that's what he told me. He lived in Puerto Rico with his mom, who had left his dad. She met another guy. Apparently he hit them. One day she couldn't take it anymore and she kicked him out."

La Manuel took a sip of water and continued.

"One day, El Bori was coming home from school and he heard his mom screaming. The door was open, he ran in. His mom was being stabbed to death, right in front of him. He doesn't remember anything after that. Not the burial, not what happened to the murderer. He went from foster family to foster family. Then from juvie to juvie. Until he got to New York and he started going from shelter to shelter. That's when we met that night near Port Authority. He told me all this once and we never talked about it again."

We sat in silence.

"I'm going to sleep. I'm tired," said La Manuel.

"Okay. I'll stay here. I'm going to lie down on the sofa for a while."

"Go to sleep if you want. I'll make some coffee when I wake up. I don't feel like it right now."

"Me neither. I don't feel like coffee."

La Manuel went to her room. I turned off the living room light and lay down on the sofa. Outside, the wind pounded the windows. El Bori said the wind in Chicago was brutal. It could practically sweep people into the air. At least between those four walls, El Boricua wouldn't have to turn his back to the wind again.

Lorena the Chilena

⟡

THE LAST AFTERNOON I spent with Lorena, we went to eat at Juanita's, the Boricua restaurant at 48th Street and 9th Avenue. It was Sunday. We had money in our pockets, as we always did after a weekend of hard work.

"My treat.

"No, *my* treat."

"*Ay, loca*, please."

"Okay, fine. You treat me to dinner and I'll treat you to dessert later."

"We won't be having anything *later*."

"I was just talking about some *flan*."

"Oh. I thought you were talking about another kind of dessert."

"You mean the white stuff we're having after dessert?"

"*Qué lesa que eres.*"

I loved when people called me *lesa*. It was like going back to Chile after so many years. Lorena and I were *paisanas*. She left her town, Villa Alemana, at the end of the sixties. I heard her talk more than once about going to see performances of the Blue Ballet in the hills of Valparaíso. They were a kind of dance troupe who played female characters. They wore false lashes made of tinfoil. Lorena said you could see them glimmering on stage. She often repeated this story with a nostalgic lilt in her voice. She left Chile in the years when I was just an infant. Many years later, when I arrived here at the end of the nineties, we ended up meeting.

Lorena was the one who taught me where to find *empanadas*, *sopaipillas*, and even chicken *cazuela* when I felt homesick. Every once in a while, when she wanted to get clean, she'd admit herself to Saint Clare's Hospital. I always went to see her there. Lying back with an IV in her arm that delivered a solution to clear out her system, she'd ask me to go pick up two beef *empanadas* from a *fuente de soda* across the street run by a Chilean woman whose name I think was Rosa. If I told them I was there on behalf of Lorena, they always threw in two cheese *empanadas* on the house and said they'd treat her to some *picarones* next time she came around in person. So many smells washed over me just hearing those words. Aromas that opened into memories. Just like Lorena, Doña Rosa wanted to go back. She told me once that as soon as she turned sixty-five, she'd go back to Valparaíso, to a house she'd bought in Cerro Alegre. Since she was an American citizen, she could claim her retirement check from anywhere in the world. That way, to use her words, she could dedicate herself to *la dolce vita*.

On that last afternoon, Juanita's was packed. We sat down at a table in the back. I ordered the grilled chicken breast with extra onion, yellow rice, and black beans. All Lorena ordered was a small chicken soup.

"That's all you want? I told you, it's on me!"

"*Ay, no*, thanks. I'm still sort of high. I was sewing a cape for Francesca. I had to get it done last night, so the *loca* had to give me a little you-know-what to keep me awake."

"I'm sure I have no idea what you mean."

As soon as I said it, we burst out laughing.

We capped off our feast with an order of *flan*. I devoured it. Lorena only had two spoonfuls. I paid the bill and we started to walk uptown. It was summer and night was falling. The streets were bustling. The nice weather here is so fleeting that New Yorkers always take as much advantage of it as they can. Music and voices could be heard until dawn.

Walking through Columbus Circle, we made eyes at a couple boys walking by.

"*Ay, loca*, did you see that *boricua*?" Lorena asked me.

"Yeah, Puerto Ricans are next-level gorgeous."

"True that, and I remember I used to be in love with an Ecuadorian."

"I never knew you were in love with a *ñaño*."

"You better believe it, *niña*. How do you think I cooked you that professional-grade ceviche the other day at Melanie's?"

"*Uy, sí*. That's right. With the tomato sauce and everything, can you imagine."

"Well that's what I made for my husband every weekend. When I didn't have to go work in the factory, obviously."

"What factory?"

"I did sewing for some Koreans. There must have been thirty of us sitting at our sewing machines. Sometimes we'd work twelve hours with no break. Technically our shifts were eight hours, but the Koreans always asked if we could stay late. If anyone said no, they'd usually get fired a few days later."

"I'm surprised you didn't start hustling like all the other girls."

"*Ay, no.* One time, Vivian, this girl whose shows I used to make dresses for, invited me out to the bar at Sally's. That place on the first floor of the Carter Hotel, *acordái*? Back then I was already living as a woman 24-7. And I was on a full dose of hormones, so I looked gorgeous, gorgeous. I'd left Hugo back in Chile, so from then on I was always Lorena. Mind you, I always sewed the name Hugo Loren Design into all the clothes I made. To represent all that I am."

The fresh breeze, which swept through the streets looking for bodies to envelop, chose ours. Sirens from a passing fire truck brought us back to New York's asphalt reality.

"Like I was saying," continued Lorena, "Vivian, who in addition to doing shows was also picking up tricks at bars, introduced me to a guy and told me to take him upstairs. She said he was staying in the hotel and he'd give me a hundred bucks. I hadn't even managed to say yes or no when *bam*! I was with the guy in the elevator going up to his room."

"And?" I asked her, with a trace of morbid curiosity.

"*Ay, no*, the guy wasn't even handsome. It was a tough pill to swallow, if you know what I mean. Fat, pale, one of those guys who smells like puke. You know, a human vomit. You can imagine what happened next. On top of it, AIDS wasn't an issue yet, so no one was using condoms. That experience was my debut and my finale as a prostitute."

"Let's go over and sit in Central Park, and you can give me a little dose of life and love," I proposed as we passed the statue of Christopher Columbus.

"A little dose of mortality, you mean."

"I guess it's all the same."

We went into Central Park and sat down on a concrete bench under some hundred-year-old trees. I thought of how we must have looked from afar, like part of some great work of art.

"You're the lookout," she told me.

"Okay," I said, standing up and switching into radar mode.

She did a bump and handed me the bag. Then I sat down and she stood up to be the lookout. I did a bump. We sat down side by side.

"That's what I'm talking about, *weona*," she said, looking at me, and we both started to laugh. "How many years has it been since you were in Chile?"

"Almost ten."

"Girl, that's nothing. I've been away more than thirty."

We were silent for a moment.

"Do you miss it, Mona?"

"Sometimes I do, sometimes I don't. You?"

"Yeah, sometimes. My mom turned ninety a few months back. I sent my sister two hundred bucks to throw her a little party. I sent her a dress, too. It was pink, her favorite color."

"Did they send you pictures?"

"I don't like seeing photos. I'd rather imagine what they all look like now. It's been so long, I don't know if I'd even recognize them."

When I think back and remember the energy of that

moment, I know we were both thinking the same thing. Night had fallen, people were headed out of the park, and the new fauna were coming in.

"Look, I think those two are cruising," Lorena said.

"Definitely. I was into cruising back in Chile. I'd go to the parks, up to Santa Lucía hill and the Lira underpass. Not anymore, though. I like peep shows better. Less walking around. It's faster and more direct."

"I'm all about the gays-for-pay at Port Authority."

"*Oye*, I feel like we're getting stuck here. Let's keep moving," I said, standing.

We left the park and walked a few blocks uptown along Central Park West so we could turn toward Columbus Avenue. Lorena wanted to see if she could find anything interesting over there. She often went around the streets of Manhattan looking for stuff people had thrown away. She found all kinds of things, from Broadway costumes to Chanel handkerchiefs to Lancôme makeup. Even a black-and-white checkered jacket with a Bloomingdale's label that she gave me one Christmas. I still have it, to this day.

We walked slowly to 46th and 9th, where I was renting a room. Back then I lived with Francesca, Melanie, La Fernando, and La Vivian, each one of us in her own room.

Lorena was our habitual guest. She'd stay one night in one of our rooms and the next night in another.

When I moved to Washington Heights, our visits were few and far between. I heard Lorena moved to a hotel on 52nd Street between 9th and 10th. I heard that once, in the middle of Manhattan winter, on one of those nights when the streets were full of snow, she decided to go out to the grocery store in the middle of the night. They told me that, either on her way to the store or on her way back, her heart said *basta* and she collapsed. She had an ID on her, so it was easy to identify the body and get her information. It turned out she had family in Canada who dealt with the body.

I like to think that they cremated her and sent her ashes to Villa Alemana. That they left Lorena under the tree where little Hugo would kneel to pray as a boy. Never again did I see Doña Rosa or eat another one of her beef *empanadas*.

A Coffee Cup Reading

WAKE UP DESPERATE. I know what I'm doing. I've been lighting candles for years. Floating folded-up scraps of paper with his name and my name in cups of water sweetened with honey. I'm in love. As soon as I wake up, I dial the number.

"Hi, Niña. It's me. I need you to do a coffee cup reading. I can give you five bucks today and the other five on Friday." Before I hang up, I add, "And could you make me a little cup of coffee, *por favor*? You're a doll."

I get up. I go to the bathroom. All I do is brush my teeth and wash my face with cold water. I get dressed quickly. I pull twenty dollars out of my wallet. I walk toward Niña's, which is less than two blocks away. I stop by the bakery. It's eleven in the morning. It's still early, I think, as I go in to buy the last of their fresh bread. I pick up my phone again.

"*Oye*, Niña. What kind of bread do you want? Just in case you feel like making me some fried eggs, too."

I ask the Dominican girl behind the display case for two loaves of *pan de manteca* and one loaf of *pan de agua*.

When I arrive at the building, I don't even bother to see if the elevator's working. I climb the five flights in a matter of seconds. The door to the apartment is already open.

"Niña!" I call out once I'm inside.

"What's up?" a voice answers from the kitchen.

I zoom down the hall and stop right in front of Niña. She's sitting next to the window that looks out onto St. Nicholas Avenue. She looks at me with her big, dark eyes. She holds out her hand.

"Give me the five dollars."

Once I sit down, I take the bills out of my pocket and

give them to her. La Niña snatches them from my hand and stands up from her chair.

"Be right back," she says.

"Wait, I brought bread for us to have with the eggs."

"Calm down. You're super anxious. Take some water out of the fridge. It's chilled. I'm leaving the door open. Don't lock it. I'll be back soon."

She exits quickly. Running, I might even say. I stay seated. I breathe deeply. I stand up to look for a cup. I find a large, clear one made of glass. I fill it with water that I take out of a gallon jug in the fridge. I drink slowly. It's ice-cold. It refreshes me. It relaxes me. I sit down again. I feel a sense of calm surrounding me. There's seriously something special about the water at Niña's house. From where I'm sitting, I look at the window that opens to the street. I see the church across the way. It's a concrete church, unpainted. Niña lives on the fifth floor, so all I can see is the cross. Far off, I can hear the sound of traffic. The flapping and cooing of a few pigeons who come to rest in the window snaps me out of my daze. I sense the apartment door open.

"I'm back," says Niña, walking toward the kitchen. "Have you simmered down?"

"*Ay, sí.* There's something special about this water of yours."

"That's the truth," she says as she smokes.

"I brought some *pan de agua* and *pan de manteca.*"

"Okay, pass me the eggs from the fridge. They're going to be delicious."

"Your eggs always turn out delicious," I say, opening the fridge and passing her the eggs from the upper compartment. "I'm going to have some more water."

"Of course, *bebe.* It's good for you. I'll do your reading after you eat."

For a moment there, I'd forgotten why I came. My anxiety returns.

"*Sí*, Niña, I need a reading. He hasn't called me in a week. Do you think he's seeing some other *loca*? He always calls me on Thursday, but yesterday? *Nada.*"

I'm still talking when Niña puts a plate down in front of me.

"Eat."

I start to eat obediently.

"Mmm," I exclaim. "This is amazing, especially with the onion and tomato you put in."

My anxiety makes me forget I've also brought *pan de*

agua. I stand up, and before I finish the eggs, I grab a big piece of bread and load it with everything left on my plate.

"*Ay, Dios mío*. I love watching you eat," La Niña says, laughing. "You eat with so much gusto."

"You're just such a great cook," I tell her, my mouth still full.

"Now I'll make the coffee."

She takes a percolator coffeepot from the stove and washes it carefully in the sink. The pigeons who flew away come back to rest in the windowsill, flapping their feathers and cooing.

"Look. Pigeons never came here before. What happened?"

"No idea," says Niña, indifferent. "Okay, the coffee will be ready in a second."

In the meantime, she takes out a shiny white cup and puts two spoonfuls of sugar inside. The coffee is ready. She serves me even less than half a cup. Then she puts some in her cup. She sits down, as always, next to the window. She lights another cigarette.

"Save some coffee, so we can do your reading."

"This coffee is perfection," I say nervously as I drink it.

Niña picks up the phone and dials a number.

"What were the results?" she asks someone. "Okay."

She hangs up. I see the expression of disappointment she shakes off with a sigh.

"I know," I tell her. "Your numbers didn't win."

"Well, no. But it's okay, maybe next time."

"*Ay*, Niña, if you just saved all the money you spend on lottery tickets, you'd be rich. What you have is a bad habit."

"Everyone has their vices," she says, looking me in the eye.

"That's true," I tell her, lowering my head and remembering people in glass houses shouldn't throw stones.

We sit for a few seconds in a silence that's interrupted only by the pigeons' flapping and cooing.

"Okay, let's do this. Come closer, time to start."

I sit down in the chair facing her. She pours what's left of the coffee into my cup and says to me, with gravity, "Remember not to drink it all. You should drink three sips and leave some coffee. The first is for you. The second is for your home. The third is for the knowledge you seek."

Once I've taken the three sips and have a bit of coffee left in the cup, La Niña puts it on the stove over low heat to dry out what's left of the coffee. A moment later, she picks up the cup, puts on her glasses, and starts to look.

"What do you see, Niña? Tell me what you see," I ask her anxiously.

"I see money entering your house."

"*Ay*, please. You always say that. Tell me about him. Is he with someone else? Why hasn't he called?"

"Patience. And don't talk to me like that. The spirits will get mad and I won't be able to read anything."

"Okay, I'll calm down," I say with deference.

"Yes. Look." She shows me the inside of the cup. "See that big stain? That's him. And he's facing you. That means he's thinking about you."

"Really? So he's going to call me?"

"Yes, take a look. See those grounds in the shape of a person? It's a person of great stature. He's tall, isn't he?"

"So tall. He's six foot three," I reply, trying to make out the person who's supposedly inside this coffee dust. "So, he's going to call me?"

"Yes. Relax." She sits there looking pensive. "Either today or tomorrow he'll call."

I let out a sigh of relief. It feels as though a weight's been lifted.

"More coffee?" asks Niña.

"No, I want some more water. The coffee's winding me up."

I take more water from the fridge and sit back down. As I drink, I hear the pigeons again.

"Look, Niña, turn around. The window's full of white pigeons."

She turns around. She looks at them and says, "Poor guys. At least they're free. You know they use doves for witchcraft."

"Really? I had no idea," I tell her, surprised. I've lived in New York for many years, but some things still amaze me.

"When I was a little girl and we lived in Bonao, in the Dominican Republic, we had a neighbor who did witchcraft. One day I was out on the back patio and I saw he'd left a cage of doves open. A few of them were hanging around the patio. Some had even come over to our side." She pauses. "I thought about how they were going to be sacrificed. They were beautiful, so well groomed, well fed. They were nice and plump. Can I have some water?"

I stand up. I open the fridge. I take out the gallon of water and fill up a glass. I do all this as though it were some kind of ceremony. Niña takes a big sip.

"Like I said, the doves looked really plump. You can't imagine how bad I felt for them."

"Obviously," I say, getting ahead of myself. "You saved them from being sacrificed and they all flew to freedom. You have such a good heart, Niña."

"No way. They clip doves' wings when they trap them so they can't fly."

"So what did you do?"

"What do you think? I grabbed a few and cooked up a nice dove stew," she says, opening her big, dark eyes wide.

"What?"

"Yep, I thought if the doves were going to be sacrificed, they might as well be sustenance for human beings. So I trapped them and made some dove soup that turned out delicious."

I sit there with my mouth agape. Silently, I stand up. I need a fresh glass of water. I fill it up. I drink it all in one gulp. Then I sit down and start to laugh.

"*Ay*, Niña. Honestly, you're too much."

"Wait, that's not the whole story."

"*Ay, no*. There's more?"

"*Claro*."

"Well come on, spit it out. What happened? Did the neighbor figure out it was you?"

"*Bueno*, if you want me to tell you the rest of the story you have to go down to Habibi's and buy me a few cigarettes."

"*Ay*, Niña, don't be like that, I don't have much money left."

"Today's Friday. You'll make money at the bar. And that man is going to call you. Listen to your little witch."

I don't know if it's her prophecies or my curiosity, or a mixture of both, but I stand up and go down to the Arab guy's store to buy two cigarettes. Just as I'm about to give him a dollar for them, my phone rings. It's Niña.

"Actually, make it four. Trust me, the story's that good."

I buy the four cigarettes. And I run up to the fifth floor to hear the end of the story.

I find Niña looking pensive, gazing out at the church with her back turned to me. The cross is her across-the-street neighbor.

"I love the view from your window," I say, handing her the cigarettes. As I start to sit down, I add, "That Gothic style sometimes makes me feel like I'm in the Middle Ages."

Niña inhales deeply. She exhales with great pleasure, cleansing her throat and her memories with the smoke.

"*Mami* was the funniest," she says, laughing.

"Funny how?"

"Because of what happened with the doves."

"Oh yeah?"

"She said not to give her any stolen dove meat, she'd only have the broth."

Niña and I start laughing. I stand up to serve myself more water.

"*Ay, no.* Your mom sounds like a riot."

"The pineapple was bitter in those days."

"What do you mean by that?"

"The pineapple was bitter. Things at home were bad. There was no money. Maybe that's why, when I was on the patio out back and saw the doves, I decided it was better for them to feed a hungry family then to be sacrificed in the name of witchcraft. I grabbed them, snapped their necks once and for all, and that was it. All of us at home ate happily, especially my mom."

We start laughing again.

"Ay, my *vieja*, I miss her so much."

Niña has a big framed photo of her mother hanging in

the living room. You can see it from the kitchen. I look at her from where I'm sitting and smile.

"I need to get going. I'm going to rest and eat something and then I have to get ready to go to the bar."

"Remember he might call you today."

"Well," I tell her, "if not today, tomorrow."

We say goodbye. I promise I'll bring her the five dollars on Sunday. And if the man of my torment calls me, I'll bring her ten. I'm tired. I wait for the elevator. I go to my room. I lie down on the bed and sleep deeply. The insistent ring of my cell phone wakes me. And what do you know? It's him. He wants to see me tonight. It's nine. I'll see him at midnight, like I always do.

I stretch out on the bed and start getting ready, beginning the ritual that will leave me looking beautiful. I think of his image at the bottom of the coffee cup and of the white doves coming and going in the window. I think of Niña's mother drinking just the broth, hold the dove. I think of hunger and of love.

Mother Hen and Her Chicks

※

IT HAD BEEN A PRODUCTIVE DAY. Six clients for Diana and three for me. It was already 11:00 P.M. and we were ready for bed. We'd already paid for the motel room so we could stay another day. We were planning to get up so we could find at least as much work as the day before. The place where we were staying was near the edge of the Hudson River, in Fort Lee, New Jersey. All we had to do was cross the Washington Bridge from the bus station in

Washington Heights, and in fifteen minutes we were in the Garden State. Every once in a while, we switched up neighborhoods to look for new clients.

It was the middle of winter. The cold was intense that night, as was the heat in our room, so we had to leave the window open a crack to let in some cool air. On top of it, I'd just started on new hormones, Mexican injections known as *cuerpo amarillo*, which for twenty bucks you could get at the home of Raquel, a trans girl who lived in Queens. Every weekend she organized a party we nicknamed "the vitamins for gorgeousness party." I was having hot flashes like any woman during her period.

"The only thing I miss about Texas is the climate," said Diana, my Honduran friend, her cheeks like two red apples.

"Texas? When were you there?"

"Years ago. Before I went back to Honduras."

"What?" I asked her, surprised. "I thought you came here from Honduras and never went back to your country, just like all of us."

"No. I came here for the first time when I was eight. My twin brother and I came to live with my mom, who was living in Houston."

"So why'd you go back to Honduras? If you stayed, you'd have your papers by now. You know what it's like to be looking for tricks here in Jersey. If an undercover cop nabs us, we'll go straight to immigration prison, and from there it's a kick in the ass: back to Central America for you, and for me, off to Antarctica."

I thought my comment would get a laugh out of her. Instead, a silence followed that was interrupted only by the sound of faraway traffic. It was one of those silences that always precede a memory.

"We were eight years old. An uncle of ours who bred chickens took us across. Honestly, all I really remember is he hid us under the floor mats in a cargo truck. He put the thick, hard cloth down over our faces and told us not to move or speak unless he told us to. That's the moment when I started to miss my grandmother. She's the one who raised me."

"The one you always call on the phone?"

"How'd you know?"

"Ay, *loca*, please. It's not like we just met."

Finally, Diana laughed.

"As soon as we got to my mom's, my brother and I started going to school. At first, I didn't understand anything. But in a few weeks, I could already communicate pretty well in English, or at least I could understand everything I heard."

"And, more importantly, you were with your mom. She must have been so happy."

"I barely ever saw her. My mom worked nights, so when we left for school she was already sleeping. Sometimes she waited for us and made us breakfast. The three of us would eat together. She always looked tired."

"*Claro, mujer.* We both know working nights will destroy a girl."

"That's true. She worked so much that lots of times she would fall asleep watching TV. But, in the end, that's how she ended up paying for my brother and me to cross the border, and even a few of my uncles and one of my cousins after that."

"Sounds like your mom didn't just go the extra mile for you guys, she actually *dragged* herself the extra mile."

"You could say that," she replied dismissively. She waited a few seconds and said, "I'm just thinking about the mother hens who won't leave their chicks, no matter what happens."

"What do you mean?"

"My brother and I decided to go back to Honduras."

"But you were so young!"

"Yes. We were ten at that point. We were eight when we got here. We lasted two years in that place."

"How did your mom not say anything? After she'd paid so much to bring you over? And when you were just kids."

"My mom was in another world. I don't know that she really cared."

"What are you talking about? I'm sure she cared. And anyway, I don't know how she let you go back to Honduras."

"She was like the Shakira song: blind, dumb, and deaf-mute. Head over heels for the man who lived with us."

"Your stepfather?"

"Yeah, although I'd rather call him literally anything else."

"He wasn't a good guy?"

"He abused me and my brother."

Images and sounds of children playing at recess came to my mind. Children looking at me, children smiling. The children's laughter wasn't happy and it wasn't sad. It was the laughter of children.

"Mother hens never leave their chicks, is what I was saying."

"Maybe your mom didn't know. You said she was always working."

My friend looked pensive. To break up the silence and bring us some good energy, I said, "At least you seem to get along well with her now?"

"Yes, I don't hold it against her. We just told her we missed our grandmother and she didn't object to letting us go back."

"Maybe she knew the real reason and wanted you to be in a safer place."

"You might be right. And she was expecting that guy's baby. My brother and I couldn't wait to go back to Roatán, to my grandma's house. If he didn't abuse me on any given day, he'd abuse my brother. It was like that every day. We were so relieved when they put us on the plane to go back. It felt like we could breathe again."

"And your mom never found out?"

"No. What difference would it have made? In any case, that guy was arrested for armed robbery right after we left. They killed him in jail. I should also mention that he's my sister Rosie's dad, and I adore her. It's in the past. What's done is done."

"Who else have you told about this?"

"My grandmother. Because when I was thirteen I started drinking. I'd get home pretty drunk. I barely ever went to school. One of those nights, she confronted me. It all just spilled out."

"How did she react?"

"She didn't say anything. We never talked about it again. It seemed easier just to play dumb about that kind of thing. To close your ears and your eyes and just pretend nothing's wrong."

The silence that followed was intense.

"If that guy abused you and your brother, he must have also been abusing your mom. She must have been terrified, too."

"A mother hen never leaves her chicks."

I stood up in the darkness and went to the bathroom. I turned on the cold water in the sink. I was thirsty. I offered a glass of water to my friend Diana.

"No, thanks," she answered.

I went back to the bed.

"What color hair do you think the Virgin Mary has?" she asks me out of the blue.

I tell her I have no idea.

"I think it must be golden."

We sat in silence. I could sense from my friend's breathing that she was falling asleep. It must have been past midnight. The traffic on the Washington Bridge had thinned out. I watched Diana sleeping; she breathed like a child. A ray of golden light came through the window and illuminated the room for a few seconds.

Sabrina's Wedding

❧

"**THIS *MUÑECA* IS READY TO GO**," I say to Diana, looking myself over in the mirror for the nineteenth and final time.

"*Uf*, it's about time."

"*Ay*, it's so much easier for you, Diana, you're trans 24-7. *Travestis* have to build ourselves *de pie a cabeza* every single time. Now I'm done from head to toe."

"Isn't it about time you started your transition? You're sort of behind."

"Next year, *muñeca*. Next year," I replied, wanting to change the subject. Getting started on hormones isn't so simple, and neither are the laser hair removal and electrolysis I need to keep my beard from growing. Not to mention I'll have to get some hair growing on the old noggin.

"Let me just have the last beer," says Diana.

"That's enough. You know you're getting trashed at the party."

"*Ay*, who knows. This is Sabrina's wedding we're talking about. If she's the one throwing the party, anything can happen."

"Don't be a bad-luck bird. Everything's going to be fine. Today our *loca*'s getting married, so she'll be in a good mood."

"Mm-hmm, very high and in a very good mood," says Diana, making noises with her nose as though inhaling something.

"Speaking of which, you wouldn't happen to have a little something for my nose, would you?" I ask her, touching up my false lashes.

"*Ay*, don't even bother. You know I don't take that stuff. I just keep some around in case a client wants some. But if you want to give me a hundred bucks, I'll give you a bag."

"*Ya, loca,* I'm not one of your tricks."

"Then forget it," she says dryly, looking at her phone. "Ready? The taxi will be here in less than ten."

"*Sí,* more than ready," I say, taking my twentieth and final look in the mirror.

"Let's go, then."

She tips up the bottle to drink what's left of the beer. Before we leave, she comes over and asks me to pose with her while she takes photos with her cell phone.

"I'm going to put them on Facebook. I'll photoshop them later in the car."

We walk out of her apartment and take the elevator. We walk down St. Nicholas Avenue, where Raimundo, Diana's personal taxi driver, is waiting for us. My friend isn't just your average escort. She's an escort who charges so much she can afford to have her own personal driver.

It's the end of September and a soft breeze heralds the fall.

We take the West Side Highway. I've always liked to ride that way in a car. Especially at night, when you can see all the skyscrapers lit up to one side and the lights of New Jersey on the other. It's daytime, but the grandeur of this city still amazes me and makes me feel sheltered, protected. Despite all the terrorist threats, I feel safe in New York.

In less than twenty minutes, we're at Penn Station. We have to take a train to Long Beach.

We walk through halls jam-packed with people. Some of them look at us with curiosity. Diana flirts here and there. I'm not feeling it, I'm in movie star mode, rocking the rather fake Versace glasses I bought on Broadway in Upper Manhattan.

At the booth, we buy a one-way ticket. Once we get there, we'll work something out with the other *locas* to split a taxi back to the city. Honestly, with the high we'll be riding, we'll be in no condition to take the train.

They announce over the loudspeakers that our train is about to depart. We run frantically to the platform, and the second we step onto the train, the doors close behind us. We sit down in the back, where there are barely any passengers. Protected from indiscreet looks, we attend to our respective housekeeping. Diana, who has a long career behind her, knows all the tricks. Instead of going to the bathroom, she drops her pants right there and carefully tucks her penis and testicles into her tiny pair of panties. After running for the train, I'm sweating more than a little.

I take out the paper towel I always keep in my wallet, take off my wig, and dry off my sweaty scalp.

I'm just beginning to relax when the guy appears who checks tickets. I'm happy to see this forty-something white man dressed in a uniform that, even in today's technological world, hasn't changed colors or styles in decades. He belongs to the group of city dwellers that withstand the passage of time. They've always been around.

We hear them announce that the train will stop at every station until we arrive to Long Beach, our destination.

"This sucks. I was hoping we'd go express," I say, annoyed, to Diana.

"Actually, that's better. Gives me time for a little nap, to make up for last night. I barely slept."

"Go for it. I'll wake you up before we get there."

I get comfortable and touch up my wig. I can't let myself relax so much that I fall asleep. I know I'll leave the seat covered in makeup.

As the train winds along its route, I think about how great Sabrina must be feeling right about now. She's getting married today. I imagine her running along the beach, dressed all in white, holding the hand of her new husband, tossing her veil up so that it falls at the ocean's edge, all wet and immaculate. I try to imagine my face on that person's body instead of hers, dreaming that I'm the one getting married.

I'm about to let out a sigh when they announce Long Beach is next. I wake Diana and she sits up, stretching her arms.

"Are we already there?" she asks me, her eyes still closed.

"Almost. It's the next stop."

We stand up, and when we arrive, we exit the train. We're greeted by a breeze that blows both warm and cool. You can feel how close we are to the ocean. Diana says we should look for a taxi.

On the street is a line of taxis with drivers reclining in their seats, listening to music or a baseball game. They look pretty relaxed. The polar opposite of Manhattan, where they act like piranhas when they're looking for passengers. And now that Uber's around, they're worse than ever. We climb into the first one in line.

"To the beach," I command.

"What part of the beach?" the driver asks with his white guy from Long Island look.

Diana and I stare at each other.

"We're going to a friend's wedding," we say like robotic twins.

"Oh! I know where that is," he says. "Lots of couples get married in that part of the beach."

"If not, we'll just follow the scent of queens' feathers burning." We laugh along with the taxi driver, who definitely has zero idea what we're talking about.

And that's where we go. Through an area that seems like a neighborhood. To our right and left, only trees and houses. After driving for a few minutes, we come to a road lined with vegetation. All of a sudden, in front of us, the sea appears.

"Leave us here," Diana interrupts.

"Really? You sure?"

"Yes. Let's walk along the beach a little. I haven't done that in ages. The *locas* should be around here somewhere. I'll just call one of them with my cell phone. We'll find each other with GPS."

"Of course. I always forget you're a twenty-first-century queen."

The taxi driver charges us twenty dollars. Diana pays him, we get out of the taxi, and she immediately tells me I owe her ten.

While our driver takes off, we stand there in silence, savoring the ocean breeze. We inhale and exhale. All that's missing from this beach is the chatter of seagulls. Sometimes I forget this ocean isn't my native Pacific. All of a sudden, we have the strong urge to throw ourselves into the sand and not to get back up again. We're about to let ourselves fall when we hear laughter in the distance.

"Did you hear that?"

"Yeah, hold on." She looks for her cell phone in her purse. "Let me call Cassandra. Hi. Yes, it's me, Diana. I'm here with Monalisa."

The wind carries over another echo of laughter. Not just any laughter, but—we would know it anywhere—the laughter of *locas*.

Diana stays on the phone with Cassandra.

"What? Let me see. I see the veil over there, the wind's almost blowing it off. Sounds good, I'll see you in a second."

There's a veil in the distance. That must be where we're going, where Sabrina's getting married. I think we must be late; the party's already started.

"Cassandra says something happened, we'll find out when we get there."

As we approach, we hear the laughter more clearly. The

sea breeze is exquisite. Our friends toss up the veil and let it fall slowly, with the velocity of the wind. They try to catch it only to throw it back up again. Like a child's game. Cassandra, Pamela, and Candy. Just three women who, with their extravagant laughter, simulate a multitude.

"Where's the bride? Gone on her honeymoon already?" I ask, noticing Sabrina isn't there. Everyone stops laughing.

"She's sitting over there," Cassandra says, looking toward the water's edge.

As I walk over to Sabrina, I hear someone behind me saying her fiancé never arrived. It sounds like Candy's voice. Sabrina's sitting in the sand. I sit down beside her.

"He didn't come."

And in the style of a Mexican *telenovela*, she tilts up a bottle of tequila and says with irony, "It's Patrón, of course. If we're getting drunk, it better not be on just anything."

"Give me a sip."

"What about I give you a bump instead?"

"Girl, please. What kind of question is that? You offend me."

She gives me a bump. She does one, too. We look out at the blue ocean. Sabrina is dressed all in white.

"*Oye*, that dress is spectacular."

"You think so? They sent it from México."

"Let's see, stand up. I want a better look."

I help her up. The dress is incredible.

"It's hand-sewn," she says, twirling and twirling.

"It looks expensive."

"Obviously. How dare you, Monalisa. Do another bump and take another tequila shot."

"Okay, but this is it. I want to be in my right mind so I can really enjoy this place."

"You're right, *vieja.*"

"*Vieja* your grandmother."

We start to laugh again as we do the last bump and drink the last sip of tequila. In silence, I assume my role of legendary *loca* or, should I say, vintage queen. I lean in, give her a tight squeeze, and tell her this is just one of life's many challenges, that a woman who carries her fan wide open sometimes has to pay the price. And not to get too down, because when it comes to men, there's more where that came from.

It must be after eight, evening time. The breeze is still warm and the light from the sun turns yellowy, orange.

"Listen up!" Cassandra shouts out of nowhere.

Someone's playing a song on their iPhone. We start to

listen to *"Como la flor,"* sung by Selena. We go back over to Pamela, Cassandra, Candy, and Diana, and we start to dance. "Just like a flower was all the love . . ."

"Where's the veil?" I ask, realizing it's missing.

"Gone with the wind," says Sabrina, somewhere between relaxed and smiling.

We laugh and we dance until the sun goes down. From a distance, we must look like a coven of multicolored witches.

ABOUT THE AUTHOR

Iván Monalisa Ojeda was born in the late '60s in southern Chile and grew up on the shores of Lake Llanquihue. He/she studied theater at the University of Chile, in Santiago, and when he/she got his/her degree, Iván Monalisa settled in New York, where he/she currently lives. He/she published an essay collection, *La misma nota, forever* (Sangria Publishers, 2014), and has written articles for magazines and plays. In addition to being a writer, he/she is a performer and is at work on a novel. He/she lives in Washington Heights, New York.

ABOU

Hannah Kauders

from Boston. She

American culture

in fiction from Cc

undergraduate w

have appeared in

Journal of Litera

the 2020 Iowa Re